DROPPING IN

DROPPING IN

GEOFF HAVEL

 FREMANTLE PRESS

First published in 2015 by
FREMANTLE PRESS
25 Quarry Street, Fremantle 6160
Western Australia
www.fremantlepress.com.au

Reprinted 2015.

Cover design by Ally Crimp.
Cover image courtesy of The Power of Forever Photography.
Printed by Everbest Printing Company, China.

National Library of Australia Cataloguing-in-publication data

Havel, Geoff, 1955- author.

Dropping in / Geoff Havel.

ISBN 9781925162219 (pbk)

For children.
Friendship--Juvenile fiction. Skateboarding--Juvenile fiction. Cerebral
palsy--Juvenile fiction. Attention-deficit hyperactivity disorder--
Juvenile fiction.

A823.3

Publication of this title was assisted by the Commonwealth Government
through the Australia Council, its arts funding and advisory body.

Fremantle Press is supported by the State Government through the
Department of Culture and the Arts.

For
Mandy Lesk, Terrence Phillips, Gavin Spriggs,
David Reynolds and my son Josh
who all inspire me to have a go no matter what.

I must also thank Peter Bistrup-Hall
who I met nine chapters into writing this book.
When he rolled into my physiotherapist's waiting room
he was the complete physical manifestation of the main
character I'd been imagining.
His advice and enthusiasm have been a massive
influence in the shaping of this story.

1

I'm PlayStationed to death and I'm watching the street for entertainment. Drizzle smears the window. Shades of grey smudge into each other and run down the glass. The house feels like a cage.

Across the street a person is framed in a watery yellow square. It's a kid looking out — like me — except his head is wobbling all over the place. He sort of tips it back and then it nods forward on a different angle. I can't see his eyes but I know he's watching, checking out his new neighbourhood. The furniture van was just leaving when I got home from school yesterday. I didn't see any people arrive so maybe he came in the night. I wave but he doesn't wave back. He turns on the spot and slides out of sight. That's what it looked like, sliding, not walking. Weird! I watch for a little longer but he doesn't come back.

Right then, the phone rings. It's Ranga. He wants to come around and have a game on my PlayStation. PlayStation again! I feel like screaming. But knowing Ranga, he'll think of something crazy to do. He always does and then we end up in deep trouble.

'Righto,' I tell him. 'See you soon.' At least I won't be bored.

I go back to the window and watch Ranga running the hundred metres up the street from his house. He runs through the deepest puddles he can find. When he gets closer I can see him grinning. The idiot! But he's having a ball, sploshing along with his feet flying out sideways. Classic! I'm grinning, just watching him. It's been like this since I can remember — since I can remember anything at all.

When he turns into our driveway he leans over like a speeding motorbike. I can't hear him but I bet he's making engine noises. It looks like he's changing gear as he passes the letterbox, his hair plastered all over his forehead.

I jump up. He won't just make wet footprints on the floor; he'll make major puddles all through the house. I grab a towel from the pile of unfolded washing on the lounge and meet him at the front door.

'Hey Sticks,' he yells, like I'm kilometres away instead of just in front of him.

I hand him the towel. 'Dry yourself before you come in.'

He scrubs his head with the towel, making his hair stand up like it's on fire. Then he laughs. 'How badly do you want me to kick your butt?' He grabs the PlayStation controls and boots up a game. Somehow the PlayStation is fun again.

I've totally massacred Ranga in three different games and he's dead meat in this one when Mum walks in. A frown darkens her face when she sees Ranga. He has that effect on adults. It takes an effort, but she forces a smile.

'Hello Warren,' she says pleasantly.

Ranga doesn't look up. He's concentrating so hard on the game he hasn't even heard her. I kick him. Lucky he sees Mum before he says anything.

'Hi Mrs Whyte,' he beams at her.

He's got absolutely no idea that she doesn't like him. In fact he'd be amazed if I told him that most adults don't like him. He's got no idea at all. He can be really aggravating, but I know what he's really like. Yesterday he gave his lunch to a little kid who forgot to bring any to school. Ranga went hungry. I'd already eaten mine so he couldn't share with me but he didn't hesitate. And he'd do it again tomorrow — no worries.

Mum's been shopping and she needs a hand to bring everything in. Ranga's out the door before I can stop him. Sure enough he tries to carry too much and drops a tin of marmalade on the driveway. The rim is dented. Mum looks at it for a while. I think she's about to say something but her face changes when she sees the look on Ranga's face. He looks like a puppy expecting to get smacked.

She shrugs. 'We can always open it at the other end, Warren.' She smiles and I can feel Ranga's relief radiating around the kitchen. She pulls out a tin of Milo and a pack of Milk Arrowroot biscuits. Dip and Gunk. Excellent!

While Mum is making the Milo we argue over the rules. Ranga's always trying to figure out ways to cheat but I'm onto him. I rule out every suggestion for changes that he makes. Then we play scissors paper rock to see who goes first. Ranga loses. He always does. I can read him like a book.

He has to go first, while his Milo is still boiling hot. He holds the Milk Arrowroot biscuit between his thumb and forefinger, loosely, letting it swing a little over his steaming Milo.

He's deadly serious, frowning with concentration,

waiting for me. I click the stopwatch. 'Go!'

Ranga plunges his biscuit into the Milo.

'Past halfway!' I say.

'It is!' he snaps. 'Quiet!' The frown grows deeper. A wet stain creeps up the biscuit from the Milo. Just above the surface of the Milo the biscuit begins to swell

'Ten seconds,' I say.

Ranga's hand shakes slightly. The biscuit wobbles like jelly. The secret is not to hold it too tight, otherwise it snaps off on the edge of the dry part.

'Fifteen seconds!'

Smoothly Ranga lifts the biscuit out of the Milo and raises it to his mouth. It bobbles around like pale-brown gorilla snot. Just as he gets it above his face a crack appears where the swollen wet biscuit meets the hard dry part, then the wet part drops straight into his mouth. He swallows it whole and grins. 'Your turn.'

Fifteen seconds — the record for this game. It should be easy to beat.

Ranga clicks the stopwatch. I put the biscuit into my Milo so carefully that I don't stir it at all. I've put extra sugar into mine so it's thicker and won't soak into the biscuit as easily. I can't lose.

Ranga tries every trick in the book to put me off but I

am focused. At fifty-five seconds I open my mouth.

'Sixty,' says Ranga. He's laughing — the mongrel!

I force away the smile that tries to creep onto my face. I lift the biscuit. It's huge, bloated with Milo — wobbling. I swing it up towards my mouth. In slow motion the crack appears. It widens and then the bottom of the biscuit drops away from my hand. I try to get my mouth under it but it brushes past my chin, splurts down the front of my shirt and splatters all over the table.

'Ha!' Ranga's on his feet pointing at me. 'Gunk!' he yells. 'Gu-unk!'

I smear the remains into a pile with my hands, then I pick up a spoon and scoop some into my mouth. I screw up my face, pretending it tastes bad, swallowing as though each spoonful is a brick.

Ranga is laughing so hard he's hugging himself. 'Urgh — gross.' He acts like he's vomiting so I pretend some of it wants to come back up and I squish a bit of mush out between my teeth. Ranga's eyes are watering.

'What do you think you're doing, Ian?' Mum's standing by the edge of the lounge room, hands on hips, glaring at me.

I wipe the goo from the corners of my mouth with the back of my hand. 'Dip and Gunk,' I say.

She stares at me and then at Ranga for a second. It feels like eternity, then she spins on her heels and heads out into the backyard. 'Clean it up!'

Ranga's got his hands on his hips, head jutting forward, chin out and eyes glaring. 'Yes, clean it up!' he says, pointing at the gunk. 'You dirty boy!' He spins around twice like a ballet dancer and stalks into the lounge room, leaving me trying not to crack up and spray gunk out of my mouth.

I've just got to the sink and rinsed out a dishcloth when Ranga calls out to me. 'Hey Sticks, there's a new kid over the road.'

I wipe up the gunk. 'Yeah,' I say. 'I saw him just before.'

'Does he live there?'

'I think so. New people moved in last night.'

Ranga comes running into the kitchen. 'There's something weird about him, the way he was sitting there. I think he saw me but he didn't wave. He just went.'

I nod. 'It was the same before, when I saw him.'

'He looked like a retard.'

I have this uncomfortable feeling, like something bad is going to happen. Ranga just said what I thought when I saw the kid, but I didn't say it. Not out loud anyway. I know what Mum would say if she heard me and I can't let Ranga say it either. 'Don't say that. You don't know what's up with him.'

Ranga just shrugs and picks up the PlayStation controls again.

2

It's a typical Monday morning. We're in home group just wasting time before our first lesson when the door opens. Mr Sutton, the principal, pokes his head in. 'I've brought the new student, Mr Brown,' he says.

Mr Brown jumps up. He looks guilty. I bet he was playing Angry Birds on his laptop. He nods. The principal steps into the room, holding the door wide open.

There is a whirring noise and one of those motorised wheelchairs edges its way through the door.

The kid in it is our age. His head is tipped forward and sideways. His hand on the control joystick is clawed and twisted. I can tell he is concentrating as hard as he can to steer the chair. He's pretty good at it because he makes it into the room without crashing into anything. He drives to the centre of the room and turns to face the class.

The principal clears his throat. 'This is James,' he

says. 'I'm sure you'll all make him welcome.'

A sort of smile flashes over James' face but it disappears as quickly as it came. He is concentrating on the wheelchair controls again, except he can't seem to look directly at the joystick. His head seems to want to turn to the side all the time.

Mr Sutton nods at us as if to say, 'Come on, where's your manners?'

'Good morning James,' we all chorus.

'Goo mooning,' he slurs. It sounds like he is fully drunk.

The classroom falls silent. We are all staring at James, wondering. And then a voice rings out in the silence.

'He's a retard!'

The whole class takes a breath at once.

James flinches. There's a hurt expression, a flash of anger and then he grabs at the joystick on his wheelchair. He's having a lot more trouble getting hold of it than he was just a second ago. His face twists up all over the place and there's tension shaking his arm. He goes red as he tries to force his hand to grab the joystick, but it won't obey him. He leans forward and puts his eyes close to it. Then he has it and he turns the chair on the spot and heads for the door. His wheel scrapes the frame on the way through.

Mr Brown gapes for a second and then he takes off after him.

'McEvoy!' Mr Sutton's face is white. 'Get — to — my — office!'

Ranga's face is like an open book with blank pages: no expression at all, like he can't understand what just happened.

'McEvoy!'

Fear comes creeping into Ranga's eyes. It's in the way his head sinks into his shoulders. It's in the bunching of his mouth. He knows he's gone too far this time but I bet he doesn't know why, even now. Mr Sutton called him by his surname. Usually when Ranga does something stupid and gets into trouble Mr Sutton calls him Warren.

Ranga nods. 'Yes, Mr Sutton.' He walks out, head bowed — condemned.

Mr Sutton turns to the class. 'Don't ever,' he waves a finger in the air, 'ever let me hear anyone say anything like that again.' He pauses, staring us down. It takes a couple of seconds before he's satisfied we are all scared enough. 'James has cerebral palsy. He's not intellectually challenged — not retarded like Warren called him. He's as clever as any of you.' Mr Sutton gives me a heavy look. It feels like he thinks I had something to do with what Ranga did. Then he says, 'James' body just won't obey his brain properly.'

I'm trying to imagine how that must feel, what it would be like, when Mr Brown steps back into the classroom. 'Mr Sutton,' he says softly, 'can I have a word with you?'

Mr Sutton nods and steps outside. He's still half visible, talking to Mr Brown, so no one speaks. We just look around at each other.

Finally they both step back inside and right behind them comes James. He drives over to the middle and turns his chair so he's facing the class. He's been crying. His eyes are red and puffy.

All I can think of is how brave he is. For once Mr Sutton hasn't got anything to say.

'This way, James.' Mr Sutton hovers over James as though he's his mother or something. He leads him through the class to Ranga's desk, the desk next to mine. He drags Ranga's chair out of the way and James parks his wheelchair there. 'Ian will show you around,' he gives me a meaningful stare, 'at recess.'

James gives me that quick smile again. Is it really a smile or just a random expression on that face of his?

'Cool!' he says.

He seems happy to sit next to me, but does he recognise

me? Does he know Ranga was around at my place yesterday? How would he feel if he knew I was actually wondering whether James was slow before Ranga blurted the thought out? I'm really uncomfortable. I don't know where to look but then home group ends and we have to go to maths.

I walk beside James and he tells me about himself. He used to live in Townsville. His father is in the army and he's been transferred to the SAS base in Swanbourne. He says it was hot up there and it feels freezing here. He slurs some words and stutters a bit but it's easy to get what he's saying.

I'm agreeing about how cold it has been here lately when he says, 'It didn't stop your friend from jumping in the puddles.'

Jeez! He does know! I'm trying to think of something to say when we arrive at maths. I make a big deal out of finding a seat just to get out of talking for a bit.

Turns out he's good at maths. He answers lots of questions and he gets the answers right too. He's pretty brainy.

I end up hanging out with James all day. It's okay but if I have to do it every day it'll get boring. James can't do much.

Ranga doesn't come back to class. I bet he got suspended.

3

It's nearly dark. Mum will be calling me in for dinner soon but I don't want to go in yet. Ranga still hasn't come out of his house. Maybe I should go down and check on him. Trouble is, Ranga doesn't like me to go down there. Nearly every time I say we should go to his house for a change, he says we can't because his mum isn't well. I've only met her a couple of times but she seemed alright to me.

I don't know why I should be worried about someone seeing me looking at Ranga's place but, as I start walking down the hill, I'm acting as though I'm just going for a stroll in the evening. You know — just casually looking around at the scenery. The cold air nips at my ears and I hunch my shoulders so my hoodie covers more of my neck. The streetlights come on before I even pass my neighbour's place. It gets dark so early in winter.

As I walk past Ranga's house I steal a glance at the front window. Yellow light leaks through cracks in the blinds, all warm and homely, like he's in there in his PJs, about to have dinner. I nearly turn around but I force myself to walk up to the house. I have to see how he's doing.

I'm almost at the front door when I hear his mum shouting. She's yelling that Ranga's a nuisance and that he makes her life miserable. There's some scuffling and a crash and suddenly the front door is ripped open. It's Ranga's mum. She steps outside even though she's in a dressing-gown. Her hair is all messed up. She's breathing heavily, like she's puffed. I think she's trying to calm down.

She stops when she sees me. She stares at me for a second and then kind of pulls herself together, like all her joints were loose and she is tightening the connectors. 'Warren can't come out,' she says. 'He's grounded.'

'For what he did at school?' I ask.

She just stares at me. Her eyes are red.

'It wasn't really his fault,' I begin, but she interrupts.

'Don't you defend him!' And she slams the door shut.

I stand there for a second as though I expect something else to happen but everything is quiet. I don't know what else to do so I head home. I'm walking up the hill when a car toots. It's Dad, home from work.

As I reach our letterbox I look across at James' house. He's in the window, like last night, but this time when I wave he waves back. If it wasn't dinnertime I could probably go across and talk to him. But it is, so I don't.

As we eat dinner I tell Dad about what happened. He doesn't ask questions as I speak. He just nods every so often. It's good telling him stuff. Mum always tries to take over your story, asking questions and telling you things about the people you're trying to tell *her* about. Sometimes she makes you forget what you're saying. Tonight she doesn't interrupt either. Once she lifts her hand and leans forward, but Dad catches her eye and shakes his head. She looks at him for a moment and then sits back and lets me finish.

When they've heard everything they try to tell me about James and cerebral palsy, but they don't really know any more than I do. They say how sorry they feel for James, but I get the feeling that they are sorrier for James' parents than they are for him. They say how hard it is for them and how Mrs Davidson has had to give up work for all these years to look after him and that it is very expensive to look after a child with cerebral palsy and how they have to have a special car and modify the house.

After a while it starts to annoy me, Mum and Dad going on about how hard it is for James' parents. I just know that I'd hate to be him, stuck inside a body that won't obey you. I've only known him for one day but they're talking about him like he's a problem, not a kid.

'He's not a problem,' I say. 'He's James.'

Mum and Dad look at me and then they look at each other.

'Yes,' says Dad. 'Yes, of course.'

4

I'm walking to school down the street. Ranga usually waits for me on the front porch of his house, sort of hopping up and down on the spot. It's as though he's got overcharged batteries and all the extra energy is sparking out of him, making him bounce. Today he isn't there. Maybe he's still suspended. I slow up and look for signs of him at the windows. Nothing. Then just as I pass the driveway he calls to me. 'Sticks! Wait up!'

Me waiting for him — that's a change! Ranga walks down the driveway and straightaway I know something's not right. He never walks anywhere, he runs. He's got one arm tucked up against his side as though it's sore. His bag is on his other shoulder but he's leaning over as though it's really heavy, though it can't be — not the way it's bouncing.

I wait until he catches up. He looks tired and one eye

is puffy. It might turn black next week. He's probably walked into a door or something like that. He's always hurting himself.

'What happened?' I ask, looking at his eye.

'Nothin'!' he says. 'It was an accident.'

He keeps on walking, slowly, looking at the ground. I try to speed him up by walking fast but he just drops behind so I slow down and walk beside him. I try walking slower than him to see what he'll do but he slows down even more so I give up and just match his speed. He doesn't even look at me. After about thirty metres I can't stand the silence anymore but I don't know what to say so I just keep on walking, looking across at him every so often.

I can't work out if he is sad or angry, dragging himself along like that with his face like thunder. I'm stealing one more glance at him and just as I do, he looks at me. I just blurt out the first thing that comes into my head. 'Have a prang on your skateboard?'

'Nuh.'

'Your bike?'

He looks at me, like he's angry now. 'Why?'

'Your face,' I say, 'and your arm.'

'It was an accident,' he snarls. 'My fault, so leave it.'

Jeez, what did I do?

After sport we have to have showers. Ranga usually runs around with no clothes on, flicking everyone with his towel as they get changed. No shame! But today he's in the toilet. I change slowly and in the end it's just him and me. Finally I'm changed too and Ranga hasn't even started. He's still in there. I know he's not using the toilet 'cause there's no sound, so he's most likely just sitting.

'You'll be late for class,' I call out.

'You go,' he says. 'I'll be there in a minute.'

'Mr Brown will be angry,' I say.

'Well you better go or you'll be in trouble too.' He's getting mad again, just like this morning.

'Okay,' I say, and I start walking back to class. Whatever's going on isn't my business. At least I figure it isn't my business for about twenty metres, but then I just have to know what's going on. I turn back and slide through the door. I lean my face around the change-room wall, silently.

Ranga is struggling to get his T-shirt off. It seems like it hurts to lift his arms up. He's got his back to me as he tries to pull it over his head. He gets stuck with his elbows jammed in the armholes and his head half in and half out of the neck hole. I can see what he has been hiding — a couple of huge mottled bruises, like he's been run over by a truck.

Ranga must have heard me then, because he jumps a bit and starts trying to pull his T-shirt back on properly, to cover the bruises. His head is stuck. It looks like he's scored a goal at soccer, except he trips over the bench and falls across it. He'll hurt himself more if he keeps struggling like that.

'Ranga,' I call, 'It's only me.'

He freezes, but then, after a moment, he just pulls his shirt back down. It's amazing how it goes on so easily after the huge struggle he was just having, but that's what always happens when you're hurrying too much. Things just don't work out.

His face is all red but he doesn't look angry now — just embarrassed. He's looking at me as though he's expecting me to say something. I don't.

He does up his shoelaces and then he looks straight at me, full in the eyes. It makes me feel weird. He's too close and staring. I look at the wall behind him, over his shoulder.

'Don't tell anyone,' he says, all low and fierce, but kind of pleading.

'Tell them what?' I ask, but I think I know.

'You know!' he growls.

I nod. But I don't really. I just have an idea I don't want to think about.

'I was being stupid,' he says. 'I'm sick of it, that's all — sick of being me. I'm sick of the stupid things I do.' Then he just gets up and walks to maths.

Now I'm not sure exactly what he wants to be kept secret.

At the end of the day he's not waiting at the front of school. I hang around to see if he got detention or something but he doesn't turn up. He's gone without me.

5

James is looking across at my house again. He's not behind his window like usual. He's on the front verandah. I'm inside looking back at him from behind the curtain so he can't see me. I don't want to be friendly after school today. It feels like he caused all of Ranga's problems and Ranga is my friend so I should be mad at James. The trouble is I know that's not fair. James didn't do anything.

'What are you doing?'

I jump like I've had an electric shock. Mum's voice is normal but I feel like she just leapt out at me and shouted. My fingers are tingling.

Mum walks to the dead centre of the window. 'What are you looking at? Oh, it's your friend James.' She waves at him.

My friend? James? It's another surprise — thinking that James might be my friend. I hardly know him. If he's my friend, why am I hiding from him?

'Looks like he wants to play,' Mum says. She's looking at me kind of funny.

I think I have to say something, explain why I'm still behind the curtain, but I don't know why. James must know I'm here now, and anyway, what has he done except be friendly to me?

'I'll go over for a bit,' I say. I have to do something.

'Okay,' says Mum.

James is still on the front verandah of his house when I walk down our driveway. He's smiling. I can see it from here. It's a big happy smile. He's happy to see me and I don't know how I feel.

I glance down the road at Ranga's house and then I cross over.

James rolls his wheelchair forward a bit as I walk up the steps. 'Hi,' he says.

'Hi,' I say back. Then we both just start looking around. I don't have anything else to say. I don't think James does either.

I'm starting to feel really stupid when he says, 'Do you want to see my room?'

His room is down the back of the house. I follow him there. He drives his wheelchair fast: a bit too fast

I reckon. There are chips out of the plaster on all the corners — the same height as the footrest on his chair. I imagine him banging into everything like a bumper car at the Royal Show. It's a funny idea but it can't be right because he doesn't hit a thing all the way through the lounge room and down the passage to his room. Maybe he only sometimes loses control or misjudges corners.

His room is set up so he can get around easily. James coasts down to his desk. He judges it well, stopping just before he crashes into it. The desk is extra high so he can get his legs underneath it when he is sitting in his wheelchair. He edges forward, a bit at a time, until the desk is pressing against his chest. If he ever crashed into it quickly I reckon it would almost cut him in half.

He boots up his computer and double clicks on a game icon. It's one of those games that make you think, a quest game where you have to collect things and use them to solve puzzles and get to the next level. I don't usually play those games because I get impatient. I'd rather drive a virtual car or fight someone with swords and guns.

James is trying to get the cursor to point at a bag of food so he can collect it. He keeps overshooting and trying to move back over it but he just overshoots again. Perhaps I should help. I reach for the mouse but James snatches it away from me. He looks angry.

'I'm doing it!'

'I was just …' but James cuts me off.

'You can't just take over!' He turns back to the game, but his hand is shaking worse than before. 'It's a stupid game anyway,' he says.

His eyes are watery like he's almost crying and I feel bad because I did something wrong but I didn't mean to. He's just blown up over nothing at all and I feel like I've got pins and needles in my hair and up my nose. I mean, I just tried to help. He should be saying sorry, not me. And then he does — sort of.

'People always try to take over, like I can't do anything at all. They think they're helping but they're not.'

I don't know what to say so I just go, 'Sorry,' and sit there for a long time saying nothing. Then James hands me the mouse.

'Do you want a go?'

'I'll wreck your game.'

'There was a save point not far back so it won't matter.'

Bewdy! I click on the food bag. A little hunger graph at the top of the screen turns green and goes down. That's got to be good. Not being hungry, I mean.

'Now what?' I say.

'We need to find a key so we can open the door to the library.'

'What for?'

'To get a street directory so we can find our way around the city,' James says, like I'm a little kid.

'So where do you reckon it is?' I'm walking the avatar around the room. If I click on a spot it walks there, like Michael Jackson doing a reverse moonwalk. I'm just going around in circles. It's frustrating. I want to do something but I can't. There aren't any hotspots. I head for the door. It's shut. The avatar just stops, facing it. I can feel James watching me. He isn't saying anything. I back up the avatar and run at the door but it just stops in the same place.

I turn around to see what James is doing. He's just watching me. 'What do I do?' I ask.

He smiles. 'Type "open door" in that box at the bottom of the screen.'

I do and it does. Doh!

We keep playing and at first James has to tell me how to do everything, but after about an hour I've pretty much worked it out. It's a tricky game and I'm sick of having to think all the time. I want to shoot something or drive a car or something. It's frustrating but James is having fun. He's smiling and laughing so I play for a bit longer. James seems to want to keep going on forever but I've had enough. Eventually I say I've got jobs to do and head home.

As I walk across the road I glance down towards Ranga's place. Maybe he'll come over later. That'd be good.

6

I love Saturdays. The whole weekend stretches out in front of me. Ranga and I are skateboarding on my driveway. He's still sore but not enough to slow him down. The sky is blue, no jobs to do. Sweet!

Our driveway starts out steeper near the house and then flattens out nearer to the road. It's good fun, but there are little edges in the brick paving that sometimes catch your board a bit. If you fall it's like landing on a cheese grater so I'm wearing knee and elbow pads. Ranga's just wearing jeans. I try to tell him, but he reckons it will never happen: not to him anyway.

He is much better than me at skating. It took me ages to do an ollie and I still can't get very high. I've got lumps on my shins from trying kickflips and when I ride fakie it feels wrong. I even get speed wobbles when we skate down the hill but Ranga looks solid either way, and he can do all sorts of tricks that I can't. When he's flipping and spinning the board it's hard to see how he does it and when he lands the board's always right way up under his feet.

'Loosen up,' he says. 'You've got to take a risk to learn a new thing.'

Yes, but I want all my skin and I hate pain.

Ranga wants to enter a competition at the skate park next term. He goes up there, every so often, to use ramps and do grinds and stuff, but there'll be lots of big guys there today and we don't feel like riding that far anyway so we practise here.

He gets me to watch a freestyle routine that he's going to do. He says he'll fit it in over the ramps, easy. He's got a map of the park in his head and he just skates it in his mind. One trick joins into another all up and down the driveway. I reckon Ranga will be famous one day if he doesn't die trying something dangerous first.

'Hey Sticks,' Ranga yells. 'That kid's watching.'

James is in the front window of his house. I wave and he waves back. Then he backs up his chair and heads towards the door.

Ranga stops skating. He looks unhappy.

'What?' I say.

'Is he mad at me?'

'He's never said anything. I don't think so.'

James' front door opens and he drives out. He's waving as he comes down the driveway. 'Hi Sticks. Hi Warren.'

'Ranga,' says Ranga.

'Hi Ranga,' James says. He smiles. Then Ranga is smiling too and, just like that, we're all mates.

Ranga tells James about the skating competition and shows James his tricks. As Ranga leans into a turn James leans his head. When Ranga does an ollie James does this little lurch upwards in his chair. He's feeling every move in his mind but his body just isn't going to cooperate enough for him to do it in real life. From the look on James' face he wants to skate a lot more than I do. It's unfair that he can't.

Then, like always, Ranga has a random idea.

'I reckon I could build a ramp down here.' He points to the edge of the driveway. 'I could get speed down the driveway, ollie onto the ramp and get some serious air out onto the road.'

I can just imagine the dodgy ramp he's going to build. He'll hit the ramp and even if it doesn't collapse he'll skin himself alive and break some bones when he hits the bitumen.

I try to talk him out of it. 'What about cars?'

James pipes up. 'I'll keep lookout.'

What's James doing? Doesn't he know what's going to happen if Ranga goes ahead with this? I have to stop them. 'We haven't got any materials,' I say.

'You know how Big Rubbish Day is coming up? Well, around on Caledonia Avenue there's one of those pine pallets out on the lawn already. We could take it apart and make it into a ramp.'

'Do you reckon the wood's strong enough?' I say, trying not to sound like a wet blanket.

'Those pallets carry bricks,' Ranga points out.

So that's it. The three of us head down to get it.

James' wheelchair is very cool. He keeps up with us if we don't walk too fast. There's no footpath on our road. It's not busy enough or wide enough and halfway down to the roundabout a car comes. James keeps on going like his chair is a car too. The real car just passes him. The driver even indicates and gives James a wave as he goes by.

After the roundabout, there's a footpath. There's a gap in the curbing and the footpath slopes down to the road so people with prams can cross the road without having to go over a step. The sloped bit is quite steep and James leans his head forward before he drives up it. His chair tips up on quite an angle and then lurches level again. For a second I thought it might turn over but it's fine. James has done this before.

Down the hill, past another roundabout, and up along Caledonia for fifty metres and there's the pallet. A man is weeding his lawn. Ranga marches up to him and says, 'Can we have the pallet?'

The man smiles. 'Go right ahead.'

'Thanks,' says Ranga.

He watches us pick it up. Ranga gets on one side of it and I get on the other. It's heavy. 'Gunna build somethin', boys?' the man says.

'A ramp,' Ranga says.

The man looks worried. 'For bikes?' he says.

'No, skateboards,' Ranga says.

'You'd better double up the boards. They're too thin for that. They'll flex and snap.'

I can see the advice go in one of Ranga's ears and out the other. 'Thanks,' he says, nodding like he really listened.

Walking twisted sideways with the pallet between us is hard. We put it down and rearrange ourselves. I follow Ranga and he follows James, like a little procession.

We stop for a rest at each roundabout and halfway up our hill. When we finally get to my house my fingers are red and there is a groove across them where the edge of the pallet was digging in. Ranga is flexing his fingers and rolling his shoulders too. We're both sweating. James is fresh as a daisy.

Just for a second I think a motorised wheelchair would be a good thing. Then I see James trying to straighten out one of his legs which looks like it is trying to cramp up. It obviously hurts him. No, the chair is cool but cerebral palsy is a terrible price to pay for one.

We're too hot to build the ramp just now so we stash the pallet around the side of my house and go over to James' house to play on his computer. His mum gives us glasses of lemonade and Kingston biscuits. Between the three of us we get James' avatar to the next level and then we head back to build the ramp.

Ranga seems to have a plan in his head. He won't let me or James measure anything or suggest any changes. I reckon he thinks he's one of those handymen on television. Whack a bit off here, join it there. Easy! The nails go in without bending and the whole thing goes together straight and strong: except ours doesn't. It's a bit crooked and wobbly, with bent-over nails hanging out all over the place. When I push on it, the boards flex in the centre.

I shake my head. 'It's dangerous. It'll break as soon as your skateboard hits it.'

'No way! Look!' Ranga stands in the middle of it and bounces. I can almost see the nails working loose.

'I'm not going on it.'

Ranga starts making chicken noises and flapping his arms.

'I don't care what you say,' I shout. I hate it when he calls me chicken. I turn to James. 'What do you reckon?'

'I can't skate,' he says, 'but if I could, I'd give it a go.'

'Don't do it, Ranga,' I say. I'm almost pleading and I hate myself for it 'cause it sounds like I'm scared, but I know what's about to happen. I've seen it before.

Ranga stands at the top of my driveway, near the carport. 'Any cars coming, James?'

The road's clear. James shakes his head and Ranga's off. He pushes off with his right leg, twice, and then he crouches ready to ollie on to the ramp. He lands on the exact middle of the ramp and it flexes, but it doesn't break and it seems to spring him into the air. He gets about a metre into the air but he can't land it properly and he takes a couple of steps, falling forward with his legs kicking up behind, before forward-rolling across James' lawn. I can't believe his survival reflexes.

James is hooting his head off. Ranga's head swells. He jumps to his feet, grabs his board and runs to the top again.

The third time he lands it properly but on the fourth there's a loud crack from the ramp as he takes off. We check it out but everything looks okay so Ranga gets ready for jump five. He's going to do a grab this time.

He pushes off and gets set early, but when he hits the ramp everything goes wrong. I can't tell exactly what happens even though I'm standing there watching. The ramp seems to fly to pieces and Ranga cartwheels through the air. Somehow he gets his feet down first and breaks most of his fall before he lands on his back on the road. Then his skateboard smacks into his face. His eye is swelling before he even sits up. What's amazing, there's no grazes on his elbows or shins, just a bit of a rough patch on one hand and one shoulderblade.

Mum gives him an icepack to put on his cheek. Then Dad puts a bit of wood down outside the door and it makes enough of a ramp for James' chair to get in through our front door so we can watch telly for a bit.

Ranga pretends his prang didn't hurt much but when he gets up to go home he's limping. You'd think he'd learn, but he doesn't.

7

I'm in maths when the PA announcement comes through. 'Ian Whyte, please come to the principal's office immediately. Ian Whyte to the principal's office immediately.'

Oh crap! What's going on? I don't think I've done anything wrong lately. I think back over the last few days. Nothing: nothing worth a trip to the principal's office anyway. So what is it? My guts are squirming. What if something's happened to Mum or Dad?

The secretary at the front office looks up as I enter. She smiles, but it's not a happy smile. I can't quite work it out, but at least she's not stern — more sympathetic. I nearly freak out. Something's happened to Mum and Dad. I'm sure of it.

'Have a seat, Ian. Mr Sutton will be with you shortly.' She picks up the phone and speaks softly into it.

In less than a minute Mr Sutton comes out and walks across to me. I'm nearly choking with fear. He's going to give me the bad news any second now. I grip the chair.

The first thing he says is, 'You're not in trouble, Ian.'

It *is* my parents! Maybe Dad had a car crash. Maybe Mum had some sort of accident. Hideous possibilities rush through my mind. 'Has something happened to Mum and Dad?' I blurt out.

Mr Sutton looks surprised. 'No,' he says. 'Why ever would you think that?'

A hot relief is flushing through me when I see Ranga. He's sitting on a bench outside Mr Sutton's office, talking to some lady. I've never seen her before but she doesn't look fierce. She's leaning towards him talking softly, like she wants to help him with something. Ranga is leaning away from her like she's a spider.

He glances up as I pass. I've seen that look before. It's the look he gets when he's been accused of something he didn't do and he doesn't know what to do about it. It's an about-to-explode look. Then I'm in Mr Sutton's office.

Mr Sutton asks me to sit down in one of the chairs in front of his desk. He sits down on a chair facing me — not his chair behind the desk, a chair near mine.

'Now Ian, you're not in trouble. What we'd like,' he pauses for a second and looks towards the door, 'is your help.'

My help? We? He's the only one in here. He must be talking about that lady out there: the one who's freaking Ranga out. Who is she? What does she want?

'We want to ask you some questions relating to your friend Warren. You are the person most likely to have noticed something.'

I'm about to ask him what he's talking about when the lady walks in. Mr Sutton introduces her as Ms Broadacre. She's from some government department, some kind of social worker. She has this concerned look on her face but she looks sharp too. Her eyes stare. I have to look away and then look back. She's still staring. It creeps me out.

She sits in a chair next to me. 'Ian, your friend Warren may need help but I have to determine what course of action to take. That's where you come in,' she says.

I glance across at Mr Sutton but there's no help there. He's part of this. What's Ranga done? Do they want me to dob on him for something?

She's talking again, pinning me to my seat with those eyes. 'Several of the teachers have noticed that Warren has a lot of bruises and cuts lately. I'm wondering if you can tell me anything about them. Have you noticed that Warren has been getting injured a lot lately?'

'Yes,' I say, 'but he always hurts himself.'

She purses her lips like I've said something important and nods. 'Hurts himself how?'

I don't get it. So what if Ranga falls off his skateboard, or jumps off the roof? What's it got to do with her? I stare back but she doesn't even blink. 'He does things, you know, like skateboard tricks, and he falls off.'

'Is that how he got his black eye?'

It's like she's a lawyer and a judge all rolled into one but I still don't get what she's asking me about Ranga for. I nod. 'Yes, we made a ramp on my driveway and he was doing a jump when it broke. His skateboard hit him in the eye.'

She keeps staring at me and I feel like a bug under a magnifying glass. I shift on my chair. It feels like she doesn't believe me. 'When was this?' she asks.

'Last Saturday,' I say.

She writes in a big black notebook for a moment and then she looks up, suddenly. 'Has he ever hurt himself when you weren't there?'

I stare at her. What is she trying to find out? Then I

remember the bruises in the change rooms.

She knows I've thought of something. I don't know how, but she knows. I look across to Mr Sutton. He's definitely on her side. At least I think there are sides and they're on one side and I'm on the other, with Ranga.

I can't think of a way to tell her that explains about his bruised back in the change rooms so I just nod. I get the feeling somebody is going to get into trouble but I don't know who or even why. How can you get into trouble for having accidents?

Ms Broadacre is still sitting in her chair a metre away but it feels like she's in my face. I want to leave but I have to sit there and, bit by bit, they lever it out of me: how hurt he was, how he didn't want to talk about it, how he said it was his fault and how he said he was sick of being himself.

Then the questions aren't about Ranga. They're about his mum. What's she like? Do I see her often? Is she nice? Does she hit him? And then I get it. They think his mum is bashing him!

That's stupid! Or is it? Images flash through my mind: his mum shouting at him, the look on her face when she opened the door that day, the way Ranga wouldn't talk about it and how we never go to his house. Suddenly I don't know anymore. A sick feeling rises up in me when I think about all the things I've said. I can almost feel Ranga out in the hall willing me not to say anything, but it's too late. There's nothing I can do about it.

Ms Broadacre scribbles away in her notebook for a while and then she looks up. She leans forward and takes my hand. I recoil. I can't help it and I think about Ranga recoiling from her in the hall as I came in. What have I done? It feels like I've betrayed him somehow. She tells me that everything I've said is confidential and that Ranga will never know what was discussed in here. She says I've been a good friend to Ranga and they only want to help him.

That's all very well for her to say. Ranga might not know what I said in here, but I will. I don't feel like a good friend. I feel dirty. Even if his mum does hit him, I feel dirty.

8

It's like poison. James, Ranga and I are sitting under a tree. We're all concentrating on our ice-creams, not talking at all. I've heard a saying about this — 'there's an elephant in the room.' Well, it's like that but it's not an elephant, it's poison, and it's eating away at us. I can feel it choking me. It's there in the back of my throat and I can't swallow it or spit it out.

Ranga is staring at his ice-cream but I know he's not seeing it. I'm staring at mine but I'm watching him out of the corner of my eye. I know he wants to ask me what the lady said to me and what I said to her but, at the same time, if I was him I wouldn't want to talk about it. I don't want to talk about it either because I'll have to tell him what I said, how she got me to say things and then all of a sudden they meant something I didn't want them to.

The trouble is, Ranga and I have always told each

other everything; at least I thought we had. Maybe Ranga has had this big, dark secret he's never told me. Maybe his mum does hit him. No, not Ranga! He can't keep a secret about anything. The harder he tries the more likely he is to blurt it out.

Then he does blurt it out. 'You know that lady, the one in Mr Sutton's office?'

I nod.

'She was asking me questions, and no matter what I said, it felt like she thought Mum was hitting me. It was like being in a trap.' He stops and stares at me.

I feel relief from my fingers to my toes. 'She was the same with me. She told me she wanted to help you but she wrote stuff in her book whenever I said anything, and I don't reckon she wrote what I said.'

'Was she a social worker?' James asks.

'I don't know.' Ranga shakes his head. 'She seemed more like a detective.'

He's right. She said she wanted to help but it felt more like she was out to get Ranga's mum.

'What's going to happen now?' I ask Ranga.

'She's going to talk to Mum.'

Silence for a while.

'When?' James asks.

'Dunno. Now maybe.'

We all eat our ice-creams for a bit. What's going to happen to Ranga tonight when he gets home? If his mum is belting him he'll cop a hiding. Even if she hasn't ever hit him things are going to be bad, for the both of them. I can't imagine how bad it's going to be. What will they say when they see each other tonight?

James is the first to talk. 'I see social workers all the time. They try to help but sometimes they interfere too much.'

He stops. I wait, but he doesn't say any more. He can't say something like that and then just leave it. I can tell from the look on his face that Ranga is thinking the same thing. We're both looking at James but he's staring into outer space.

'What? What do they do?' Ranga asks.

'When I was a kid ...' James starts.

'You are a kid,' Ranga says.

'No, when I was a little kid.'

'You are a little kid,' says Ranga standing up. 'You only come up to here.' He holds his hand against his chest at the exact height of James head.

James stares at him for a second and then cracks up. We're all killing ourselves laughing and whenever we manage to stop one of us snorts and then it's on again. We can't stop until we're too weak to laugh any more.

My ice-cream has melted all over my hand while we've been laughing and I'm licking it off my fingers when James starts his story again.

'When I was a little kid,' he says. We only snigger for a bit. 'When I was a little kid, my big brother ...'

'I didn't know you had a big brother,' I say. 'Where is he?'

'He works in the mines, up in Karratha. He's an apprentice fitter.'

'How old is he?'

'He's nineteen,' James says. 'Anyway, when I was a little kid, Brad used to take me for rides on his Peewee 50 motorbike all around the farm.'

'How?' Ranga says. He's leaning forward.

'He used to sit me on the bike in front of him and put a strap around us so I wouldn't fall off, then we'd ride all around the bush tracks near our house. It was the best fun I ever had.'

'Didn't you get in trouble from your parents?' I ask.

'No, they let us do it.'

My parents would never let me do something risky like that, and I'm healthy. I used to get busted for dinking with Ranga when we were little. It was fun but we always fell off in the end, especially when we tried to stop or a hill got too steep.

James gets all serious. 'The point is we never told the social workers because Mum and Dad said they would stop us. Mum and Dad might even have got in trouble for letting us.'

'You lived on a farm?' Ranga has already lost track. 'You ever heard a baby pig when someone grabs it?' He starts sucking in his breath and making this awful screaming, squealing noise.

Jess, one of the girls sitting near us, almost has a heart attack. She jerks up and her head nearly spins off her shoulders. Then she sees that it's just Ranga. Her friends are laughing at her. She glances at them and then back at Ranga. 'Loser!' she sneers.

'Takes one to know one,' Ranga says.

Jess just shakes her head like it was a stupid thing to say, which it probably was, but what can you say when a girl calls you a loser in front of her friends?

Ranga is trying to think of something else to say when all the girls get up. It was like they had some secret signal or something. They all moved at exactly the same time. I didn't see it or hear it but they all knew it was time. Girls are like that, like a flock of birds flying, turning this way and that to some signal no one else can detect.

The girls don't walk away from us either. They go right past us in a little tight group, kind of contemptuous, but strutting at the same time. They don't normally walk like that. Why? Are they telling us something? Is it some type of lesson we're supposed to learn? It seems like they think we're all idiots and then Jess gives me this sly smile as she goes past. We watch them until they all start giggling when they walk around the corner of the canteen.

'Idiots!' says Ranga.

'You ever had a girlfriend?' James asks.

'Plenty,' says Ranga, which is bull.

'Have you got one now?'

'Nah,' Ranga says, 'I'm too busy training for the skate comp.'

'What about you, Sticks? Have you got a girlfriend?'

I shake my head. 'Nuh,' I say, but then that sly smile Jess gave me comes sliding through my mind. What was that?

James takes a big noisy breath. 'I've got a girl who's my friend.'

'Yeah?' Ranga says. 'What's she like?'

'There's a picture in my backpack, in my wallet.'

Ranga is straight into his backpack, burrowing like a wombat. It takes him about five seconds to hold up James' wallet. 'Here it is!' He hands it to James which shows a lot of self-control for Ranga. If it was my wallet he'd have it open already.

James fumbles with it for a few seconds and then shows us a picture of this girl in a wheelchair. She looks frail but her smile glows out of his wallet.

'She looks nice,' Ranga says. He gives James a nudge. 'You sly dog!'

'She's not my girlfriend — not like that. She lives down in Bunbury. We email each other all the time.'

'Where did you meet her?' I ask.

'In hospital. She was having botox injections.'

Ranga can't resist. 'No wonder she's so pretty.'

'Ha-ha, Ranga,' I say, letting him know it's a really bad taste joke.

'I don't think I'll ever have a real girlfriend,' James says.

'Why not?' Ranga asks.

James doesn't answer.

9

Mrs Jones, our science teacher, is away and Mr O'Brien, the biology teacher, is relieving.

'Turn to page twenty-six in your text,' he says. 'Mrs Jones tells me you have already covered this topic so I want you to answer the questions at the bottom of the page.' He writes the page number and the topic on the whiteboard and then sits down with a pile of marking from his real class.

The questions are boring, all about levers and forces. I bet Mrs Jones won't even look at our answers. What a waste of time.

James leans towards me. He's got his hand in front of his mouth as though he's rubbing his chin. His eye looks in danger of being poked out. 'Hey Sticks,' he says in a loud whisper.

O'Brien looks up instantly. 'James,' he says, 'Be

quiet! And get your hand away from your face. You don't fool me for a second.'

He looks down at his marking again.

'Sir! Sir!'

O'Brien looks up again. 'What is it James?'

'I need to go.'

'Go? Go where?' O'Brien's forehead furrows.

James looks down at his legs and then up at O'Brien. He has a please don't make me say any more look on his face. He does this little nod.

'Of course! Of course!' says Mr O'Brien.

'Sir!' James says, 'Can someone come with me, to help?'

O'Brien looks startled, then worried. I can almost see the cogs of his brain grinding over as he tries to imagine what a person would have to do to help James. I can't imagine anything myself, at least not anything that I care to think about. Finally he nods, 'Who would you like?'

'Can Ian come? He knows what to do.'

'Certainly,' says Mr O'Brien, looking slightly relieved.

As James turns his chair towards me, away from O'Brien, he gets the most excellently wicked smile on his face. 'So long suckers,' he whispers and he tries to wink.

I'm trying not to laugh as I follow James past Mr

O'Brien who has a concerned look on his face. I hope he doesn't decide he needs to help because then we'll be busted. Tension! Then James just thanks him and we're out. I feel like jumping and clicking my heels together as we walk down the verandah of the science wing. Freedom! But what are we going to do now? There are classes and teachers everywhere.

'So what now?' I say.

'I don't know. Anything was better than being stuck in there.'

I laugh. 'That was cool. I didn't think you would do something so bad.'

James looks sideways at me as he rolls down the corridor. 'Like Ranga would.'

'Yes,' I agree. 'But he'd get caught.'

James has that wicked look on his face again. 'I've got an advantage.' He pats the armrest of his chair and gives a bittersweet laugh.

We end up in the library reading magazines because all the computers are being used. There are a few skateboard magazines, but they're old and falling apart, with pages cut out because there were pictures or articles the librarian didn't want us to read. I've read them a few times, but Ranga has read them hundreds of times.

I reckon his hands have done half the wear and tear on the pages of this one I'm holding. There's nothing special about it: articles about a new compound for wheels that's faster and has more grip, different trucks, photos of famous skaters doing tricks and millions of ads. For a kid who can't concentrate to save his life, Ranga sure studies these. A bomb could go off when he's reading them and he wouldn't hear it.

I'm thinking about getting a book from the fiction section when James whacks me across the arm.

'Sorry,' he whispers, and then he slides his eyes sideways and tilts his head like a spy. 'Over there.'

There's another class where he wants me to look. They're doing research skills with Mrs Dearle. She's got the smart-board going. It's something to do with the UN. We'll be doing that on Thursday. One of the girls at the back gives us a little wave. It's Jess. I wave back before I even think about it. She smiles. Shit!

James is grinning at me like an idiot.

'What?' I say.

'She likes you.'

Lucky for me the siren goes.

James and I each head to our next class.

'I'll see you after school. Ranga is meeting me out the front by the bus stand,' I say.

James nods.

I've got no idea why I have to learn French but the next hour passes quickly and, at home time, we meet out the front, load up James' wheelchair with our bags and head off home. At first we talk about the day at school but then we run out of things to talk about and James motors on ahead. Our bags swing off the back of his chair as he bumps over the uneven paving.

When we're nearly home, as we come around the corner at the bottom of the hill, he stops and calls back. 'You've got a visitor.' He points towards Ranga's house. There's a car in the driveway.

Ranga stares, frowning.

'Is your dad visiting?' I say.

He shakes his head, still frowning. 'Dad's still up north. He won't have his access visit until next weekend.'

By the time we're halfway up the hill we can see the writing on the side of the car — Department of Community Services.

'I bet it's that social worker from school,' I say.

Ranga is freaking out. 'Shit!' he says. 'Oh shit.' He

keeps repeating it, over and over again under his breath. I've got second-hand butterflies in my stomach.

We're walking slower now but before we get to the house, two people come out and get in the car. One is that Ms Broadacre and the other person is in jeans that look wrong on him. He should be in a suit.

Ranga's mum is standing in the doorway watching them leave. She looks angry and she's been crying. Even from here, I can see her panda eyes. Ranga grabs his bag off the back of James' chair. 'See you guys,' he says. He doesn't even look at the social workers in the car as he walks up to his mum. She grabs him in her arms and hugs him, tight, like she'd just found him after he was lost.

They both stand there watching as the social workers drive off. When the car goes around the corner at the bottom of the hill, Ranga's mum kind of shrivels up. Ranga turns her around and steers her into the house. He gives a little low wave as he shuts the door.

'Do you wanna play my new computer game?' James says. 'It's a skateboarding one.'

I look at Ranga's house, and then mine. There's nothing much else I can do so I nod and off we go.

The skateboard game is cool, but it's not like the real thing. Nothing is as good as the real thing.

James can't play this game that well, but he keeps trying and trying, even when his avatar gets injured almost straightaway every time. He's never going to get any good. He just can't work the controls properly. His hands won't do it.

'Why'd you get this game?' I ask. 'All your other games are puzzle ones.'

'I like skateboarding,' he says.

Then I put my foot in it. 'Yes, but you can't skateboard. And this game doesn't work for you either.'

As soon as the words are out of my mouth I want to take them back. I meant to point out that this game didn't suit him, because it was a reflex, handling sort of game, but I know that's not what James hears. Just for a second he looks like I've slapped him, but then he gets this determined look on his face. 'I just want to do it, that's all.'

'But it's too hard,' I say. I'm trying to explain what I meant.

'Everything is too hard,' James says. 'If I didn't just try stuff anyway, I'd never do anything.'

I try to change the subject. 'What do you reckon will happen to Ranga and his mum?'

'Some things you can't do anything about. You've just

got to keep going and see what happens.'

He looks sad and I wonder who he's talking about: Ranga or himself.

10

Outside, the street looks just the same as it did last term but it's not. It's different. Then again, maybe it's not the street that's changed — it's my life. I'm the same as always, but everything else about my life is getting too hard and I just don't know how to sort it out.

Ranga first: he's my oldest friend and he needs help, but I don't know what to do. Nothing that I can do would be useful anyway.

James is my friend now too, but he takes up so much of my time that I can't hang with Ranga as much as I used to. Besides, he can't do a lot of the stuff Ranga and I like to do, which sucks for him. I can't do anything about that either. Being friends isn't something you choose. It just happens.

Then there's Jess. One after the other, her friends keep telling me that she likes me and she wants to go out with me. I think I like her. I mean, I like it that she likes me, and I think she looks pretty hot but I haven't really talked to her. If I do ask her out, where am I supposed to take her and what are we supposed to do? I haven't got much money — any really. I spent most of the money I did have on new skate shoes. Loser!

I want everything to be like it was. Ranga and I think of something fun to do, then we do it and it's fun. We get busted, but it's worth it. Simple!

Outside, sunlight is belting down. It's already glaring off the windows of Dad's car. The sky is electric blue like summer, except the lawn is green and I know that if I walk outside it will be cold. I love winter days like this, so what am I doing sitting around here? Maybe Ranga's mum will let him out today. We could ride down the skate park. Yes, today feels like the sort of day where I could finally get some serious air and land one or two of them too.

I should go, but I'm still sitting here, looking out of the window, wondering what it would be like to kiss Jess.

'Why aren't you out getting some exercise?'

I nearly have a heart attack.

It's Mum. She's standing right behind me. 'Why aren't you doing something with Warren or James? Are you feeling sick?'

'Why should I be feeling sick?' I ask.

'Well, let me see,' says Mum, pretending to think for a while. 'It's a sunny Saturday and you're in the house, sitting still and looking out of the window.' She puts her hand on my forehead, pretending to take my temperature. 'Oww!' she cries, blowing on her fingers.

'Ha-ha!' I say as sarcastically as I can. It doesn't work on her any better than it does on Ranga.

'Well?' she says.

'I don't think Ranga can come out at the moment,' I say.

'What's he done this time?' Mum asks.

'Nothing!' I say, maybe a bit louder than I need to. 'What makes you think he's done something?'

'Well,' says Mum, twice as sarcastic as I was, 'let me see. Perhaps it's because every other time he's been grounded, he did something.'

'Well he didn't this time,' I say.

'So why is he grounded?'

'He isn't,' I say.

'Then why can't he play? Is he sick?'

'No.' I don't want to have to tell Mum about the social worker and Ranga's bruises. It feels like Ranga's secret. Besides, Mum will find out that I knew something and didn't tell her, but Mum's like one of those detectives on television. She always knows if I'm trying to hide something and she gets it out of me in the end. 'Maybe he can go out,' I say. 'I'll ask him.'

As I head out the front door James yells from his house, 'Hey Sticks, whatcha doing?'

'I'm gunna see if Ranga wants to go to the skate park,' I say.

'Can I come?' James asks.

'Sure,' I say, 'but what are you going to do down there?'

'Just watch.'

Fair enough. I spend half my time watching Ranga do his stuff anyway, trying to figure out how he does it. I wait at the end of James' driveway while he tells his mum where he's going and then we head on down to Ranga's house. James' chair must be fully charged because it's a long way to the skate park. We have to go down a big hill and through an underpass and then it's still a fair way up to the shops and around behind them where the skate park is.

Ranga's mum opens the door. She looks tired but she gives us this big beaming smile. 'Hi boys,' she says. She turns around and yells back into the house. 'Warren, it's Ian and James.'

Ranga comes bounding up the passageway. It's the old Ranga back again. He's been inside too long and he's overcharged. Energy is sparking out of him. He's ready to go — now.

ll

When we roll up to the skate park all the usual guys are sitting around watching while a couple of the older guys are flying all over the ramps doing tricks I can only dream about. Even if I had the guts I wouldn't be able to do that stuff, ever. It used to annoy me, but now I guess I've just got used to it. Ranga is a bit of a hero here. The older guys treat him like he's one of them, knuckles and stuff. I'm lucky to get a grunt.

James though, they're interested in him. What happened to you? Can you move your legs? Can I have a go of your chair? He handles it well, answering their questions and not getting angry, even when they grab the controls of his chair and make it jerk back and forth. He won't let them have a go on it though.

I'm just about to step in and try to stop them before they break something when Ranga speaks up. He tells them to leave James alone, that James is his friend and they actually do leave him alone. I'm relieved because I'm scared; really scared. It doesn't take much for them to turn on you, and then one of them figures he needs to beat you up — especially if you're a small kid, or weak or a bit fat, or you're wearing green. It doesn't matter what it is, one of them will shove you around to prove how tough they are. All the others laugh like you're a waste of skin and you don't matter.

They might be leaving James alone, but this tall kid with long, greasy hair, who used to go to school a few years ago, decides that I need to be picked on. He walks across and sticks his face right next to mine. 'What are you looking at?'

I know where this is heading. If I say, 'Nothing,' then he'll get mad and say, 'Who are you calling nothing?' Then he'll beat me up.

I don't want that to happen so I say, 'My hero.'

He looks confused and all his mates laugh. That makes him embarrassed and mad — at me. He glares and I realise that I'm in deep trouble but then Ranga steps between us.

'Leave him alone,' Ranga says. 'He's just a kid. Pick on someone your own size.'

'Yeah Luke, leave him alone. He's funny,' says one of the big guys.

He still wants to get me but his mates will think he's weak if he picks on me. I can see him trying to decide if it's worth it anyway. Then he gives this fake laugh and says, 'Yeah, he's funny.' But his stare says, 'Watch your back,' before he swaggers over to the other guys.

Ranga puts on a show that day. He's upside down in the air half the time, spinning like a top as well. I've seen him do the same moves before but now he's linking them together and each one seems to give him more speed into the next one. I almost feel like not skating myself because Ranga is so good and I'm so bad. I'm sitting down to watch when he flies up the wall, flips his board into his hand, and lands lightly on his feet next to James and me.

'Come on, Sticks,' he says. 'Get into it. Today's the day.'

I'm pulling my knee and elbow pads from my bag when I hear a hiss.

'Sticks!'

It's Ranga. He's using his eyes to signal towards the others. 'Don't put those on. Not with those guys here.'

I glance across. They're looking towards us. Ranga's right. If I put this stuff on I'll make myself a target, but I know that if I don't I'll lose skin.

'Just play safe, at least until they're gone,' Ranga whispers. 'Don't do anything hard.'

It's easy for him to say. For me, everything is hard. Even on a slow hill I'll find a way to get speed wobbles and fall off. When I do, I land *hard*. Not like Ranga. The big guys are still watching. What's worse, getting picked on by those guys or skinning my elbows or knees? I can't win. I wish I'd never come!

I'm trying to decide when I hear wheels crunching loose stones on the cement next to me. It's James.

'Do you reckon my chair would handle that section over there?'

There is absolutely no way his chair could handle even the first section of the ramp and, even if he somehow made it to the bottom, he'd stack it so badly that we'd have to call an ambulance. I look at him and I can't believe it. His eyes are shining and he's ready to give it a go.

'You're nuts,' I say. 'If you try you'll find out the true meaning of pain.'

'I already know what pain is,' James says.

I glance at his legs. They're even more twisted up than they were at the start of the term. I guess he pretty much lives with pain, but why add to it?

'You'll lose metres of skin for sure,' I tell him and for once he seems to listen.

He nods. 'Yes, I guess so. I don't want to get injured before the operation.'

'Operation? What operation?'

'I'm having a pump implanted next week, to relax the muscles in my legs.'

'You never said anything about this,' I say. I'm almost accusing him, like he has to tell me everything he's doing.

James just shrugs and goes back to watching Ranga getting pretty close to flying. It's probably five minutes before he says, 'I've had operations before. They had to lengthen the tendons in my legs so I could straighten them a bit.'

'How? Did they cut them?' It's such a horrible idea.

James nods. 'But the last few years they've given me botox injections.'

He sees me smirking. 'Yes,' he says. 'I look young.'

'So why don't they keep doing that?'

'It only works for a while and the amount I need isn't good for me. The pump is supposed to be much better.'

'Are you afraid?'

James shrugs. 'I've got no choice.'

We sit a while and then he says, 'You know what my

friend and I told the nurses at hospital once, when we were getting botox?'

'What?' I ask. It could be anything.

'We told them we wanted our legs cut off. They just cause pain and get in the way.'

I stare at him. I can't believe what he said. He's got this strange look on his face and then it disappears. He laughs. 'Just joking, we were stirring up the nurses.'

I've got a horrible feeling he meant it and I can't handle the thought I'm having about what it would be like to be James so I just watch the Ranga show for a while.

After maybe five more minutes I decide to have a go at skateboarding myself, without the knee and elbow pads. I walk over to the edge of the ramp and put my foot on the back of my board with the front wheels hanging in the air just over the edge. I'm going to just step on the front and let gravity pull me down into the bowl. When I hit the bottom I should have lots of speed so I'll just turn off the top on the other side and slow up a bit before I try anything too tricky. I take a breath and step forward, the skateboard tips and I'm off.

The trouble is the skateboard doesn't come with me. The back wheels hook up on the edge of the ramp and I fall head first down to the bottom. My right knee smacks into the ground and the ramp sandpapers my palms. As I roll my left elbow cracks into concrete. My shirt saves my back but it's burning when I stop sliding. I'm lying there, dazed, when I hear laughter.

It's the older guys, pointing at me, slapping each other on the back and banging their knuckles together like Americans on TV. I feel worthless. I hate them and their stupid little gang. They feel like big men here, but really they're just losers and bullies. I hate them but mostly I hate myself for letting them make me feel like this, like shrivelling up and disappearing.

'Are you alright, Sticks?' It's Ranga. He's got my hand and he's checking it for grazes. 'You really splattered yourself. Hey, your elbow's bleeding.' He rips out a scrunched up tissue. It looks used.

I pull my arm away. 'You're not putting that on my graze,' I say. 'I'll die of snot infection.'

'Do you reckon my snot's dirtier than this concrete?' He's pointing at the ramp. It's dirty grey with a few red drops of my blood on it.

'Hey Sticks!' It's James. He's got his chair right up to the edge of the ramp. One centimetre further and he'll fall over. 'You okay?' He looks worried in between other expressions that come and go on his face. He does that when he's upset.

Suddenly I'm feeling better. My two friends are there for me. But then the worst thing of all happens. I cry. Not a lot. My eyes just water up enough for some to run down my face.

'There, there! Who's a little baby then?' It's the jerk with the long hair.

I pretend I haven't heard him. I just get my skateboard, climb out of the ramp and pick up my bag, but the crappiness of this rotten day hasn't finished yet. My bag doesn't jingle. I already know what it means, but I open it and check anyway. Yes, my allen keys are missing and I bet I know who took them. I look across at the long-haired kid. He smirks back.

I know I won't be able to prove he took them and if I try it will just give him a reason to beat me up. I shake my head and leave with Ranga and James beside me.

12

Jess is at it again. At least I think she is. All these girls keep pointing at me and whispering. I can't hear what they are saying which is really annoying. All the pointing and whispering goes on before school and then at recess too. By lunchtime I'm ready to go and ask Jess what's going on.

Then the weirdest thing happens. Lucy Jones, the most boy-mad girl in the school, comes up to me and says, 'Ian, Jess wants me to tell you that you're dumped.'

Dumped? I didn't even know I was going out with her. Now I've broken up with her. How is that even possible? Ranga is laughing. He tries to put a sorry look on his face. 'Hard luck man,' he says. 'Don't forget we're here for you.' He gives James a big nudge. James is struggling not to laugh as well.

I can feel a smile pulling at the corners of my mouth.

The more I try to stop it the more a laugh tries to force its way out of my mouth. When it spurts out of my nose I give up and all three of us are laughing our faces off at how stupid the whole thing is.

Lucy stands there looking at us with her mouth hanging open. I get the feeling this is not what she expected. She stares at me for a second then she spins on the spot and stalks back to her mates. Jess is over there looking kind of unhappy which is strange because she's the one who is supposed to have dumped me.

I hear what Lucy says to them. It is only one word. Gay.

One of the other girls puts an arm around Jess like she's comforting her and they do that flock of birds thing, turning around all together and walking away.

I'm left standing there wondering what just happened and somewhere deep down I feel like I've lost something. It bothers me all afternoon and I make up my mind to try and catch Jess without her friends after school and actually talk to her. She might tell her friends I'm a stalker but I don't think so.

James, Ranga and I are walking home and we're just about to go in the deli for an ice-cream when someone shouts, 'Hey losers!'

I know that voice. It's that long-haired guy from the

skate park. We turn around and he comes walking up to us. He's got a couple of his mates with him. They're like a gang and I just know they want to beat me up.

Ranga steps towards them. 'Leave him alone, Luke. He hasn't done anything to you.'

Luke sneers. 'Tell that to someone who cares.' He shoves Ranga hard. He must be strong because Ranga flies backwards and bangs into the wall. Then he turns to me. 'Feeling funny now, are you?'

The other two guys are standing either side of me and Luke shoves his face right in front of mine. 'Let's start again. What are you looking at?'

'A pathetic little thug!' says a grown-up voice, and a huge hand grabs Luke's shoulder and spins him around. It's the deli owner.

Just for a second I see the look on Luke's face. He's nearly wetting himself with fear. Then I realise that he's seen me see how gutless he is. He's *really* going to hate me now.

The deli owner is like a body builder or something. Ranga once told me that he was a sailor before he bought the deli. Whatever he was, he's strong. He pushes Luke away like he's a toy. 'Piss off, and take your weak mates with you.'

Luke almost looks like he's going to smart-mouth the deli owner but he doesn't. He just gives me a death stare and they strut off like they're tough guys. It would have been funny except they're much tougher than me and Luke will get me as soon as he has a chance.

'Are you alright?' the deli owner asks, but it's not Ranga or me he's talking to. It's James.

James nods. 'Thank you,' he says.

The deli owner smiles. 'No worries. It was a pleasure. I've watched those punks throwing their weight around for a while now. It was good to be able to do something about it.'

There's the ding of a bell from inside the deli and the man spins around. 'Customer,' he says. 'See you boys.' And he's off, back into the shop.

13

Ranga wants to go down to the skate park every afternoon to practise for the competition coming up. 'Come on, Sticks, those guys probably won't be down there. Some of them work.'

Just thinking about going down there puts a bad taste in my mouth. My grazes sting every time I bend my arm or my leg and it was hard to write at school today because the palms of my hands hurt so much. And those guys will be there. I'm too sore to go, I tell myself over and over — but I know that it is really fear that makes me chicken out and that makes me feel even worse. I make up an excuse so I won't have to go with him. It's so weak! I blame Mum. I tell Ranga that Mum won't let me go down there until my grazes heal and that I'm grounded until I clean up my bedroom.

'I'll help,' Ranga says straightaway.

'No,' I blurt out, 'you go and practise. The contest is this weekend. It'll take ages to clean up.'

'Not if we shove everything under the bed and in the cupboard.'

That's typical Ranga: out of sight, out of mind. He'd walk out of the house feeling clever and then think it was unfair when he was busted later. It's like he has a giant blind spot in his brain.

'Mum will know. She vacuums under the bed and she puts washing away in the cupboard.'

'Yes, but we'll be gone by then.'

'What about when we get back?'

'Oh yeah.' He looks crestfallen, but then his face lights up. 'Your mum will have forgotten about it by then. Anyway, she might not look today and then you could do it tonight.'

This is harder than I thought. Maybe Ranga wants to go so badly he'd be willing to wear the punishment later, though I reckon he just doesn't think through the consequences. 'Why don't you see if James wants to go,' I suggest.

Ranga looks cheesed off, like he knows I could go if I really wanted to, but he nods and heads over to James' house.

It's weird. Now I feel like Ranga is betraying me by going to the park with James. I want to be with them but I don't want them to find out how scared I am. I guess I want to be alone with my gutlessness. It's not fair to blame them for anything.

I watch through the window as they head off down the street. Ranga has his jumper off. He's waving it like a bullfighter cape and James is charging it like a bull in his wheelchair. They're both laughing their heads off. The part of me that wants to be with them gets stronger for a second and I stand up but then the part that wants to hide takes over and I sit down again. Then they're gone.

I actually do clean up my bedroom for a while but I soon lose interest. I try reading a book but that gets boring and I find myself flicking through pages, reading ahead of myself, and that annoys me. I'm ruining my own book. Maybe eating something will make me feel better.

I'm standing at the fridge door when the phone rings. I pick it up and say hello. There's silence for a while and then a soft girl's voice says, 'Sorry.'

'Sorry? Who is this?' I ask but there is a click and the phone goes dead.

Before I have time to think about it Mum is at the door. 'Who was on the phone?' she says.

'I don't know. They hung up.'

Mum shrugs, 'Probably a telemarketer.'

I nod, relieved. I don't want to talk about what girl might ring up and say sorry, not with Mum anyway. Still, I wonder if it was Jess. If it was, it would be strange, but kind of good. She did look unhappy when Ranga, James and I laughed at school. So who was in the wrong? Was it her and her mates for all the stupid going out stuff they were doing, or was it us for laughing?

'I saw Warren heading off down the street with James a while ago,' Mum says.

I know it's a question even though she hasn't asked me one but I don't want to talk about that either so I say nothing.

'They looked like they were heading for the skate park,' Mum says, looking at me.

I find something to study outside the kitchen window.

'Why didn't you go with them?'

'My grazes hurt too much,' I begin but Mum cuts me off with a loud snort.

'I almost need a microscope to see those. You've never let a couple of grazes stop you doing something you want to before, so why now?'

'I wanted to clean up my room,' I say and, as I'm

saying it, I realise what a weak excuse it is. No wonder Ranga looked annoyed.

Mum actually laughs at me. 'You? Clean up your room?' She seems to think that it's an even more stupid excuse than I do.

'Go and look if you find it so amazing,' I say. It's annoying having her give me attitude about my room. She hassles me about it all the time and now she's giving me grief for cleaning it. You'd think she'd just be happy.

Mum doesn't say anything else. She puts the kettle on. 'Want a Milo?'

I nod and as I'm nodding someone knocks at the front door, exactly in time with my nods. Mum's eyes fly open and she cracks up, pointing at me and at the front door. I nod. She cracks up even more. I'm laughing too as I head for the door.

The first thing I see when I open the door is Ranga's face with a fat lip and blood smeared on his cheek.

'What happened?' I ask.

Ranga talks out of the side of his mouth. 'That kid Luke was hassling James and he wouldn't stop. We had a fight.'

'Who won?' I ask.

Ranga starts to smile but then he winces. He holds

his lip and licks where it's split. 'I was winning, but then he got hold of me and he was punching me out when the other guys dragged him off.'

'Luke had a blood nose and I bet he gets a black eye,' James says from behind Ranga.

'So what happened when they dragged him off?' I ask.

'The other guys said he was gutless and to leave me alone. Jimmy, the guy who does all those balances on his front wheel, said if Luke didn't cut it out he'd have to deal with him.'

'He left,' says James, grinning like an idiot. 'We had to look out for him on the way home but he wasn't waiting for us so maybe he'll leave us alone now.'

'Why did you think you might run into him on your way home? You didn't go past the shop, did you?'

'No, but we reckon he lives around here.'

That's not good news. 'Around here? How do you know?'

'That's his tag in the underpass,' Ranga says.

'Warren!' Mum's seen Ranga's face. She hurries him into the kitchen. Before he can protest she's taken a bag of frozen peas out of the fridge and wrapped them in a tea towel. She tells him to hold it on his lip while she cleans up his face with a wet washer.

Ranga does everything she says, not complaining even when I'm certain she hurts him a bit wiping off the blood and putting Betadine on the split in his lip. If it was me, I'd be in trouble for fighting, but she would fuss over me too. She's a great mum.

Ranga looks relieved when she stops. It's hard to put together the kid who takes crazy risks on a skateboard, who fights guys a lot bigger than him and who always gets into trouble for saying and doing stuff without thinking, with the kid sitting there doing exactly what Mum tells him. He looks like a puppy.

'Would you boys like a Milo? Ian and I were about to have one,' Mum says.

Ranga's eyes light up. 'Dip and Gunk!' he says.

'What's Dip and Gunk?' James asks.

We tell him the rules while Mum makes the Milo.

We roll a dice to work out who goes first and I lose. That'll make it hard to win.

My Milo is steaming. Ten seconds I reckon, that's all I'll try for. Mum has the stopwatch. She's going to be the judge too.

I'm about to put the Milk Arrowroot biscuit into the Milo when Ranga says, 'Past halfway!' like we always do.

'Yes,' I growl. I take a few seconds to refocus.

'Hold it steady!' Ranga says just as I start to lower it again.

'Stop it! I know what you're doing,' I say.

'What?' says Ranga, all helpful innocence.

'You're trying to put him off,' says Mum. 'That's cheating, Warren.'

Ranga shakes his head. 'No, it's an important part of the game. I'd be cheating if I did this.' He bangs the table with his hand. My Milo slops around in my cup.

James has a huge grin all over his face. He loves it. He's holding his biscuit already but his fingers won't grab it properly. They're too tight and the biscuit is on a bit of an angle. It will snap straight off if he does it like that. I hold my biscuit up, above the cup, ready to start.

Mum hisses and raises a finger to Ranga. He sits back. I lower the biscuit into the Milo. One. James' eyes nearly bug out. He leans forward and bumps the table. My Milo slops up the Milk Arrowroot past halfway.

'Sorry,' James says, sitting back and making the table wobble again.

I can't wait any longer. Only eight seconds, but if I leave it I'll gunk. I lift it out and, as I raise it to my mouth, I see James watching everything I do, opening his mouth when

I open mine. I nearly crack up but somehow I make it.

'Beat that,' I say to Ranga through my mouthful of mush.

He just laughs and then winces, holding his lip. 'Easy,' he says but he chickens out after nine seconds and lifts his biscuit into his mouth. He smirks at me and does a number one sign with his finger.

'My turn,' James says. He gets his chair as far under the table as he can, but he still has to lean forward. He rests his arm on the table but the effort makes his hand shake worse than ever.

'I'll get a tray,' Mum says. She gets up and gets a serving tray from the kitchen. She puts it across the armrests of James' chair. A little frown flits across his face but she doesn't notice it.

'How's that?' She puts his Milo mug on the tray and steps back.

'Good, thanks, Mrs Whyte.' He smiles.

Mum picks up the timer and James gets in position. His hand is tense as anything and the harder he tries to keep it steady the tenser it gets. I'm afraid the biscuit is going to shatter.

Mum clicks the timer. 'Go!'

James dunks. He's been watching us because he only sinks it to halfway, but it's sort of waving back and forth and up and down in the Milo. It's going to snap off before he even gets it out. His face goes redder as the seconds tick past. At about ten seconds he lifts the biscuit out and actually gets it to his mouth. He's beaming, with biscuit mush oozing out of the corner of his smile. Ranga and I high-five him.

'Twenty seconds,' Mum says.

James' smile disappears. All three of us are looking at Mum.

'What?' she says.

'I only counted to ten,' James says. 'I don't want any favours. I want to win fairly.'

Mum is smooth, but we all know she isn't telling the truth. 'Time flies when you're having fun,' she says. We're all still looking at her. 'It seems to go faster when you're really concentrating. Besides, ten seconds is a win anyway.'

James is not convinced but I back Mum up. 'I counted to twenty — with "and" in between each one. Your brain must have been racing.'

James still isn't convinced. He turns to Ranga who looks back and then says, cool as you like, 'I wasn't counting. I was watching but it seemed like a long time to me.'

Finally James smiles. 'I win!'

'Only round one,' Ranga says. 'Now I'm really going to show you how it's done.'

'Bring it on,' James says.

Behind him Mum has a faraway look in her eyes and she's frowning slightly.

I have to go again and at one minute I get the Milk Arrowroot into my mouth without gunking. Ranga tries for seventy seconds but he gunks. James and I laugh our faces off while he scoops the biscuit mush off the table and eats it. Then it's James' turn.

He's got delusions of grandeur. He holds the biscuit in for eighty seconds but when he tries to lift it out, it barely makes it over the rim of the cup before it cracks off and splatters all over the table.

Ranga and I are laughing and chanting, 'Gu-unk, gu-unk,' but Mum looks really uncomfortable. She's holding herself back while we watch James trying to scoop up the gunk and eat it.

It's Ranga who sorts out the situation. 'Don't think you can get out of this,' he says. He scoops most of the gunk back into James' cup and hands it to him. 'If I have to eat my own gunk so do you. It's the rules.'

'Right,' says James and he takes a big swallow.

'Urgh!' He squishes some out between his teeth like he's been playing with us for years and we're all laughing our faces off.

14

James looks calm for someone being taken to the children's hospital for an operation. I'm looking through the window when the paramedics wheel him out of the house in one of their chairs and I run out to say goodbye.

James waves when he sees me coming and then the paramedics lift him into the back of the ambulance. I walk up to the door and when they finish strapping him in, and his mum and dad kiss him and hug him a hundred times, they let me hop in the back with him for a minute.

Once I get in there all the things I want to say disappear or seem kind of cheesy. How do you tell a friend that he is about the bravest person you know or you're going to miss having him around or that you're scared for him? Instead I punch him on the shoulder and say, 'Some people will do anything to get out of school.'

James laughs which makes me feel better. Maybe it

was the right thing to say after all and he feels better too. We talk for a while and then the paramedics tell me James has to go so I climb out. Before they shut the door I lean back in and tell him I'll come to visit him.

He smiles and says, 'See you there.' But then he grows serious. 'Tell Ranga I'm sorry I might miss his skateboard competition.'

How can he be thinking of that when he is about to have an operation to implant something in his body?

'It's okay,' Ranga says from behind me. He's puffing. He must have run up the hill. I step back out of the way and he looks at James for a moment. Then he says, 'Have a good holiday.'

We all crack up and then his mum hops in with him, the paramedics close the door and they take James away.

Ranga and I stand on James' driveway with James' dad, waving even though we know James has no hope of seeing us.

'Thanks boys,' James' dad says.

'What for?' Ranga says.

'For being good friends.'

Ranga looks puzzled. He hasn't thought about it at all. He's just been doing what comes naturally to him. I wish I was like that too, but I can't help thinking about everything. Sometimes I try not to think at all but then I realise that I'm thinking about not thinking. Doh!

At recess Ranga and I sit on the benches at the canteen eating a slice of cheese on toast each, like we used to before James came, but it's not the same. There's something missing. It's strange that nothing was missing before James came but now he's not here there is: same bench, same school, same cheesies, Ranga and me, but there's this hole in the air next to us where James should be.

'Do you reckon he's in the operating theatre by now?' Ranga says around a mouthful of toasted cheese.

'Maybe.'

We're quiet for a while and then Ranga says, 'You know how it's Big Rubbish Day next week?'

'Yeah?' I say.

'Well there's a couch out the front of a house around the corner from the roundabout.'

'So?'

'Well, you know how James wants to skateboard but it's never going to happen?'

I nod.

'Well, what if we put skateboard wheels on the couch, then James could sit in between us and we could go flogging down the hill from your place all the way to the park.'

'How would we steer?'

'I've got an idea for that,' says Ranga.

In the back of my mind I'm remembering the ramp he built on my driveway, but this idea seems so much better.

Just after lunch the PA system calls me to Mr Sutton's office again. I'm walking up there trying to think what I might have done. Nothing comes to mind. I'm up to date with assignments and homework, thanks to Mum's hassling, and I haven't broken any rules. Ranga hasn't done anything either, except get in that fight at the skate park, and that isn't anything to do with the school. But it must be Ranga 'cause I really haven't done anything. My guts are churning.

The lady behind the office desk smiles at me, all friendly. 'Have a seat, Ian,' she says. 'The principal will be with you soon.'

I sit over by the planter box watching people come and go, mostly just delivering messages or cashbooks from the different teachers. Everyone who comes in here talks softly. It's the atmosphere. It feels a bit like a library, except no one's reading. I feel like it's a law court and I'm about to be sentenced.

Finally Mr Sutton calls me into his office.

'Sit down, Ian,' he says.

I sit on the chair he gestures to. It's comfy, with armrests. If only we had these in the classrooms. I lean back, but only a little. You can't slouch in the principal's office.

Mr Sutton doesn't say anything for a while. He just stares at the desk in front of him, frowning slightly, making his mind up what to say, or how to say it. Finally he speaks. 'How have you been, Ian?'

'Good,' I say.

He points to my elbow. 'Had an accident?'

'The skate park,' I say.

'Trying for air?' he says.

It sounds so wrong, coming out of his mouth. He probably wants me to relax but it will never work. He's the principal and I'm a kid, in his office. He should just get it over with.

And then he does. 'Ian, it's about Warren.'

So it *is* Ranga. I feel anger rising up inside me. I sit forward. This time they aren't going to twist what I say.

'I told you, the black eye last week was from his skateboard. It happened in our driveway. The ramp we built broke and it hit him in the eye.'

'The ramp?'

Mr Sutton is acting like that social worker, trying to trip me up with stupid questions. 'No, his skateboard,' I snap. I'm angry.

Mr Sutton actually smiles. 'Yes,' he says, 'I know, Ian.'

We sit in silence for a minute. I reckon he's thinking about Ranga and his next question. I'm thinking about getting out of there.

Finally he speaks again. 'Were you there when he got the split lip?'

Split lip! Teachers notice everything! I have to be careful here. 'No,' I say, 'but James was. Ranga was defending James from a bully at the skate park.'

Mr Sutton just stares at me. It makes me feel really uncomfortable and I look away, but then I think that it makes me look like I'm lying so I make myself stare back and he looks away, down at his desk.

'You're certain?' he says.

I want to shout at him, 'What are you saying? Do you think I'm a liar?' but I don't. I just say, 'They came around to my place just after it happened.'

Mr Sutton nods. 'Thank you, Ian. You've made things a lot clearer for me.' He jots something in a notepad and I sit there waiting for a minute or so before he looks up and smiles. 'That will be all. You can go back to class now.'

I'm at the door when he calls, 'Ian!'

I freeze and then turn slowly.

He's smiling. 'I don't think Warren will have anything to worry about from now on.'

I stare at him. It takes me a few moments to figure out what he means. Then I mumble something and head back to class. It feels like a cloud has lifted. I think Mr Sutton actually listened to me and believed me. I'll have to wait for lunch to tell Ranga about it. He's got English now and I've got maths but that's cool.

I like algebra. I like getting real-life problems and making up equations and solving them. Let x equal the number of apples and y equal the number of boys. If only life could be solved like that. Then it would be easy. The trouble with life is that x might start out being the number of apples but then someone eats one, or you find out that one is rotten, or one is really an orange and all your problem-solving doesn't work any more. Still, in maths the logic is clean. You can work things out and there is a right answer that doesn't change, even if other people don't agree. Right is right, no matter what they think. Yes, maths is like a rest for my brain.

15

After school Ranga and I walk down to the house near the roundabout. I've been busting to tell him how Mr Sutton called me up to his office but there were always other people around at school. Now's my chance. I tell him all about it and when I say that I think Mr Sutton believes me he looks relieved. Then he tells me that he likes Mr Sutton.

'That's weird!' I say. 'Mr Sutton busts you all the time.'

Ranga shakes his head. 'Mr Sutton doesn't hate me. He's fair. If you do the crime you have to do the time.' He sounds like Mum and Dad.

But Mr Sutton isn't Ranga's biggest problem. 'What about the social worker?' I ask.

Ranga shrugs. 'I don't know. Mum hasn't done anything wrong. They can't do stuff to you just because they think something, can they? They'd have to have proof.'

'Well I reckon you've done a good job of proving that you are the worst accidental-self-mangler in the history of the universe.'

Ranga laughs, then he points at my elbow and hands. 'Except for you,' he says.

True, but for different reasons. I'm just bad at skateboarding. Ranga takes crazy risks.

The couch is still near the roundabout, on the verge, beside a pile of other rubbish. We walk up to it and feel the cushions. They're a bit damp. They've been outside for a couple of days so it figures. It doesn't matter because they'll dry out quick enough if we can get them under shelter. They might smell a bit though.

We knock on the door of the house and ask the guy inside if we can have the couch. He says we can as long as it doesn't end up on the side of the street somewhere. 'No,' Ranga says. 'We've got big plans for this couch.'

It's only about one hundred and fifty metres up to our house and the couch is quite light, but we have to put it down a few times because it's awkward and cushions keep falling off. The edges of the wooden frame dig into my hands and they're still tender from my skateboarding accident. It takes ages to get it home and my hands are stinging when we put it down on the garage floor.

Mum and Dad said it would be alright if we worked on the couch in our garage. Lucky they didn't ask what we plan to do with it. Just telling them we plan to fix it up seemed like enough explanation. Mum even backed her car out so we could work on it this afternoon. Doing it in here is extra good because James won't spot it from over his place when he gets back from hospital as long as we keep the garage door closed.

We need to get some wood for the steering so we head out again to scavenge around other Big Rubbish Day piles. As we walk heaps of cars cruise by with people checking out what's being thrown out. Every so often one stops and someone gets out and raids a rubbish pile. Mum always says, 'One person's trash is another person's treasure.' It's true! Some of the stuff looks really good to me. There's a wide-screen TV at the other end of our street. I want it for my bedroom but there has to be something wrong with it, otherwise why would they throw it out?

Around the block we find what we're looking for. There is a pile of wood like the stuff they use on pergolas stacked outside. There is a lady home and she tells us we can have what we want as long as we leave the pile tidy. All we need are two bits and we're set.

I want to draw a plan, but Ranga says he's got it all set out in his head. We tip the couch upside down and he puts one of the pieces of wood across the bottom, sticking out in front about a metre and a half.

'Screw that on,' he says.

'I'll measure it first,' I say.

'What for?'

'So it's even.'

'It doesn't have to be exactly perfect,' Ranga says. 'It'll work fine where it is.'

I've already got the tape measure out. It really gets up his nose. I can see him getting angry.

'It'll only take a second,' I say, measuring across the couch. 'What's half of one point nine metres?'

'Ninety-five centimetres,' says Ranga, quick as a flash.

'How'd you work it out so quick?'

'One point nine metres is ten centimetres short of two metres, so half of that is one metre minus half of ten centimetres is ninety-five centimetres.'

I fold the tape over from ninety-five centimetres and there it is — one point nine metres. And some people say Ranga isn't smart.

I mark the centre and we use Dad's drill and some screws to fix it in place.

'Now for the T-bar,' says Ranga. He grabs the other bit of wood and places it on the end, sliding it back and forth until it looks right. Then he marks his place with his thumb and grabs the saw.

I'm busting to measure something, but what? What's the difference if it's exactly one metre or not? Where Ranga marked it looks pretty right.

'Hold it!' I say.

'What?' he snaps.

'I'll mark it square.'

Ranga sighs. 'If it makes you happy.'

I'm annoyed, but I mark it out anyway. He saws it off and works out where the centre is. Then we drill a hole through both pieces of wood and bolt them together with washers in between so it will turn easily. All we need to do now is screw two pieces of wood to the back corners of the couch so we can attach the skateboard wheels there. Ranga has two spare trucks from an old skateboard and, because I can't skate at the moment, we use the trucks off my skateboard to finish the job.

When the wheels are screwed into place we turn the couch over to test it. Ranga sits in the middle with one foot on each side of the T-bar and I push him across the garage. It rolls as easily as a skateboard and it turns pretty well but if you turn it too tightly it sort of hooks around and tries to throw you out.

'Let's test it down the hill,' Ranga says.

'Not today,' I say. 'James' parents will be home soon and they'll see it.'

I'm expecting an argument but he just nods.

'Yeah,' he says, 'it's not worth the risk.' So we roll the couch down to the back of the garage and put a tarp over it.

We head inside for a drink after all our hard work. I've just got the fridge open when Mum comes in. 'Do you boys want to visit James in hospital tomorrow afternoon? I think he'd like that.'

'I'll have to ask my mum when I can go, Mrs Whyte, but I'd like to,' Ranga says, as polite as you like.

Mum beams at him.

16

Maths is boring today without James. Ranga is in ordinary maths so he's not here either. Just me!

Ranga really should be here in advanced maths. People think he isn't smart enough but he could be good at maths if he really wanted to be. Look how good he was at working out measurements yesterday. He says he can't stand having to learn about things if there's no point, and that there's definitely no point to algebra or calculus, but I reckon he just likes subjects where he can use his hands, or at least get up and move around every so often.

I remember at primary school, when he used to get bored in maths because he already knew what to do. He had to sit there and wait while the class went over, and over, and over what we were learning until everyone else got it too. Before long he'd start wriggling around and fiddling. You were supposed to go on with other activities if you finished work, but Ranga didn't like them so he'd do something else, something he thought of himself, like when he built a machine out of rubbers and rulers. When he pulled a lever on his side it pushed his sharpener on the other side of his desk. It was cool, but then the sharpener fell off the desk and burst open. Shavings went all over the floor and the teacher made him clean it all up at recess. He missed out on running around like a maniac all recess like he usually does so he was twice as toey afterwards when we were back in class. He ended up getting an in-school suspension that day.

Today I'm the bored one and I'm looking for something else to do. I put my eraser in the centre of the desk with my ruler next to it. When I push one end of the ruler away from me the other end comes back towards me. I slide it along so the rubber is near one end. Now when I push it, it's harder and the other end goes faster and further. What if I push on the long end?

'Ian!'

It's Mr Grey, the maths teacher. He's giving me the hairy eyeball. I don't know what I'm supposed to do. Did he ask me a question? I'm looking at him and then the whiteboard but I can't figure it out. I feel my face going red, starting at my neck and working its way upwards. Help!

'Subtract ten from both sides of the equation,' someone calls out.

Mr Grey stares at me for a few more seconds and then he looks towards the back of the room. 'Thank you, Jess. It's good to see that someone's concentrating. That's exactly what you do.'

I turn around towards Jess and mouth thanks.

She smiles.

Yes!

17

The hospital is like a rabbit warren with corridors everywhere and signs that are hard to follow. Mum seems to know what she's doing though, so Ranga and I follow her along until we reach a busy nurses' station. A nurse smiles at us and points to the phone she's talking on. She puts one hand over the mouthpiece. 'I'll be with you in a second,' she whispers, loudly.

Mum's nod is as exaggerated as the nurse's whisper. I snort. Mum glares at me so I do a naughty-boy-being-told-off act with my head-bowed-nearly-crying look on my face. Ranga snorts. Mum's eyes swivel across to Ranga but now I can see the corners of her mouth twitching.

'Can I help you?' It's the nurse.

'Yes, we're looking for James Davidson,' says Mum.

'Let me see.' The nurse looks at a list on her clipboard.

'Ah yes, he's in Room 58. It's just down there on the left.'

'Thank you,' Mum says, and off we go.

When we get there a curtain is drawn around the bed and people are talking behind it. Every so often James says something but he's too quiet for me to hear what he's saying.

I'm not ready for what I see when a nurse draws back the curtain. James seems to have shrunk. His face is pale and he's lying back on the white pillows like a white shadow but he brightens up when he sees us.

Mum says hello and gives him a kiss on the cheek like she's James' mum too. Then says she'll leave us to it.

'You've got a great mum,' Ranga says when she's gone.

I nod. I know.

James looks like he's dosed off but then he lifts his heavy eyelids and focuses on us. 'Sorry,' he says.

'How did it go?' Ranga asks.

There are tears in James' eyes. 'Not like I thought it would. They said it wouldn't stick out, but look.' He hitches up his hospital gown and shows us where the implant is.

A lump the size and shape of a pack of cards is sticking out of the skin on his stomach. The corners are barely rounded off by the skin stretched over the implant underneath. No wonder he's upset.

'It's ugly isn't it?'

What can I say? It's horrible. I can't even begin to imagine having something like that inside me, let alone sticking out like that. 'Does it work?' I ask, so I don't have to tell him what I think.

He nods. 'Sort of. My legs are a bit better — I can straighten them out more. But they can't get the levels right and I won't be able to go home until they do. Dad will be at work and Mum's exhausted so I told her she could have time off from looking after me for the week.'

'Do you reckon you'll be in here for a week?'

From the look on Ranga's face he's thinking the same thing as me. He can't wait a week to show James the couch. He wants to show it to him now.

'If they can't get the pump working right, then yes.'

A nurse comes in and wraps a strap around his arm and starts pumping it up for a blood pressure test. Another nurse comes in and there is no room for us. We have to wait outside the curtain.

'Hey Sticks, why do you reckon they put drips in everyone?'

It's a good question. I haven't got a clue what the

answer is so I make one up. 'So it looks like you're nearly dying when visitors come.'

Ranga grins, brain working overtime. 'I reckon it's because the doctors are vampires and they have to replace the blood they take in the night.'

'Well I reckon they put mind control drugs in there and one day they'll put a special signal on the telly and we'll all be zombie slaves.'

Ranga shakes his head. 'It's just to make it such a hassle when you want to move that you just stay in bed instead of running around.'

I'm trying to think of a better reason when one of the nurses opens the curtain. She stares at us for a second and then one eye opens wider and the other half shuts. 'What we really do is put tracking chemicals into your blood stream so your parents will know where you are and everything you do for the rest of your lives.' She gives an evil laugh and then both nurses leave, hanging on to each other's arms and giggling.

How cool was that!

James is looking better too. They've sat him up a bit. 'You know what I'm going to do when I get home?' he says.

'What?' says Ranga, giving me this sideways glance.

'I'm catching a taxi to the marina for fish and chips.'

Ranga looks amazed. 'How?'

'There's a taxi that can take wheelchairs. The driver is a friend of mine now.'

'I haven't seen any taxi since you moved to our street,' I say.

'I normally only use him when Mum can't take me in our car.'

'Why don't you get your mum to take you?'

'I'm sick of people doing everything for me. I want to do something on my own.'

I'm thinking about the couch. Is that the sort of thing he's talking about? Maybe he won't like it. Nah! He loves skateboarding and he'll love the couch times ten.

18

'We better test it before James gets back,' I say.

'This arvo?'

'Yeah! Straight after school before our parents get home,' I say.

Ranga looks like he's just got a Christmas present. His hands go into racing driver mode, holding an invisible steering wheel. He turns it and leans into an imaginary corner.

'You steer the couch with your feet,' I point out. 'We could put ropes down to the T-bar.' It seems like a good idea to me.

Ranga shakes his head. 'James couldn't hang on to it properly. One of us will just have to do the steering. I volunteer me. You'll crash it.'

'No way,' I say.

'Well, I'll go first.'

'Toss you.'

'Deal.'

Ranga wins the toss and won't listen when I try to make it best of three, even when I call him a chicken and make noises like a hen that's laid an egg. I'm flapping my arms and scratching the ground when I hear Jess.

'Pretty good,' she says. 'You should try out for the drama club.'

I'm so embarrassed I can't think of a thing to say so I just give this stupid laugh.

Ranga glances at me, then he turns back to her. 'Hi Jess,' he says, and moves over on the bench so she can sit down. She does, but she leaves enough room for me to sit between her and Ranga.

'Not sitting with your friends today?' Ranga says.

'Nah! It's my turn to be picked on.'

I get up enough guts to sit down too. 'Thanks for yesterday,' I say. 'I was miles away.'

'Miles away?' Ranga says.

Jess laughs. 'You might as well say he was in outer space.'

'Nearly,' I say.

'Where's James?' Jess asks and when I tell her she looks so upset for him that I start thinking that she's a really nice person as well as being cool. Then I tell her about the couch and how we're going to test it out this afternoon and, before I know it, she's coming too, to be a substitute for James in the trials.

We're just organising a time to meet at my place when a flock of girls, led by Lucy Jones, comes flouncing past so obviously not looking at us that even I figure out that that's the whole point.

I look at Jess, trying to get an idea of how she feels about the way they're acting. She gives me a smile and a shrug as if to say, 'So what?' She just gets better and better. For the rest of the day I catch myself thinking about her. I don't get a lot of learning done.

We all meet out the front when school finishes and head home. Jess rings her mum on her mobile to tell her where she is. I kind of expected her to say that she's going over to a girlfriend's place but she says she's coming over to my house to work on a hill trolley. It's cool, even if she didn't mention that the hill trolley is a couch. Her mum must be cool too. I wonder what my mum would say. She'd probably be okay about it, but I'd get interrogated when I got home. I probably will anyway if Mum sees Jess with us. She won't today though — she's at work.

We're talking about all sorts of stuff as we walk along and Jess is walking next to me. Her hand is so close to mine that I start thinking about holding hands with her. Once or twice I nearly reach out and grab it but I chicken out. What if she doesn't want me to? What if she pulls it away? I'm gutless. I know it, but I don't want to wreck things. Then Jess looks across at me and smiles and I nearly get brave enough right then.

As we pass the deli I've got my eyes peeled for that guy Luke but I can't see him. I look across at Ranga and he's not worried at all. It's like he got rid of any fear when he stood up to Luke. I figure I'm too chicken to fight so it looks like I'll have to stay scared of him for a while. Then I look at Jess walking next to me and I know I want to toughen up.

All the way around the bend and up the hill I'm thinking about holding her hand and about facing up to Luke. It's like she doesn't think of me like I'm a little kid and that makes me feel grown up. It's funny how we've always been the little kids on the street and now we're older all of a sudden.

Jess has to sit on the couch because that's what James would do and Ranga is sitting dead centre with his feet on either end of the T-bar. I'm doing the pushing.

A car comes up the hill, turns right at the roundabout and disappears around the corner. It's the only car we've seen for the last ten minutes.

'Go,' yells Ranga. 'Go! Go! Go!'

I shove the back of the couch as hard as I can until it starts rolling down the hill, faster and faster. I'll have to judge it so it doesn't get away from me. Then I feel it starting to speed up on its own so I run around the side and jump onto the seat. The couch lurches sideways and starts swaying.

'Careful!' Ranga yells, holding the T-bar steady.

It works, because the couch settles and we hurtle down the hill. Here comes the roundabout and I'm feeling uneasy. What if there's a car coming up the side street?

'Watch out for cars,' I yell, but Ranga is too busy woo-hooing to hear a thing and Jess is hooting so loud it almost hurts my ears. We're going so fast by the time we reach the roundabout that we get a bit of a lean up as we go around it, first one way and then the other. After that the road is a gentle curve and we sit there, enjoying the ride, until the couch stops way down by the next roundabout.

Trouble is, now we have to push it all the way back

up again and it won't steer straight. Ranga tries lifting the T-bar and dragging it from the front but that makes the back of the couch drag on the ground. The only way to do it is to get Jess to steer while Ranga and I push. It's hard work. We're both puffing when we reach the top of the hill but that's because we hurried so we could have another go sooner.

On the next run Ranga is pushing off and I'm steering. It's not as easy as I thought to keep the couch steady but, as we pass the first roundabout, I start doing swerves from side to side and we're all leaning our heads in time with each other and laughing our faces off.

There's just enough time left for Jess to have a go at steering before we have to pack it away, otherwise our parents might show up and ban us from using it before James has a go. We charge down the hill sitting bolt upright, with our arms folded, as cool as anything, and Jess holds my hand while she steers.

Woo-hoo!

19

On Friday morning James is back at home, looking out of his window just like he used to. I give him a wave as I head down the hill. I've got my school bag over my shoulder. Ranga comes out of his house and we walk past the roundabout and around the corner acting natural. Once we are out of sight we duck down the path into the middle of the park, where no one can see you from the road, and sit on the swings waiting. After about fifteen minutes Jess comes in from the other side of the park where her house is. It's just like being spies.

We hang around, planning how to surprise James. Jess keeps looking over her shoulder so I turn around to see why. There's no one there. I'm relieved. For a moment I thought we were about to be busted.

'What?' says Ranga, looking at us both.

'It looks like it's going to rain,' Jess says.

'No way!' says Ranga. 'I watched the news last night. It's not going to rain until Sunday.' He looks confident, but then again, he always looks confident.

I didn't see the forecast but big, black clouds are building up on the horizon. It does look like it is going to rain — soon. For the next half an hour we wait, every few minutes stealing glances at our watches and then at the clouds. Ranga keeps getting up and sitting down until it's time.

At exactly 8:30 we walk back up the street. All of us are straining our eyes to see if any cars are still in the driveways of our houses but it looks all clear. Our parents are at work. Cool! James' mum is working today as well and his carer won't be here until ten o'clock so we've got an hour and a half.

The way we've got it planned is like this: Jess and I go into the garage and get the couch ready behind the garage door while Ranga knocks on James' door. When James comes out we'll press the door opener and we'll stand there with the couch like we're about to go where no man has been before. If only we had a smoke machine. Anyway, then we'll load him up and off we'll go. Ranga is going to steer for the first run. Jess and I are going to push off and I'll jump in the couch once it gets going.

Jess will get a ride down the next time while I'm steering and then she can have her turn driving.

Jess and I roll the couch to the front of the garage door. She stands next to it, ready. By the time I get to the little side door where I can see Ranga's signal he has already rung the doorbell. It seems like ages before the front door opens and James appears. Ranga talks to him for a while and then James rolls his chair out to the top of his driveway. Ranga signals like a maniac behind him.

The garage door takes a while to open but when we finally see him it's worth it. He's staring at us and his mouth is hanging open. He still hasn't got a clue what is going on but he drives his chair across to get a better look — fast.

Jess and I bring the couch down to meet him at the road, ready to go. For the first time I start to wonder if James will be keen. It would be scary to do something like this if you couldn't move your legs or arms like you wanted. I don't need to worry. From the look on his face it will be hard to stop him. He's seen the T-bar on the front of the couch and he knows what it means. In about five seconds he's hassling us to give him a ride.

Ranga gets on one side of James' chair and I get on the other. He's lighter than he looks and we lift him out easily, but when it comes to getting him down on the couch it's much harder. We have to lean forward to put him on it and the couch keeps rolling backwards. Jess gets behind it and holds it steady but even then we wind up having to half dump him like a bag of groceries and then help him to sit up and move into position. We put a cushion between him and the armrest to stop him leaning too far out that side when we turn.

Once he's set we line the couch up on the road and Ranga gets into the driver's seat, feet on the T-bar. No cars have come past since we started so we figure it's as good a time as any for our first run.

Jess and I shove the couch off and once it's rolling I jump aboard. At first it sways everywhere but Ranga holds the steering bar steady with his feet and things settle down. James is on the other side of Ranga but I can hear him hooting. It's just like I imagined but somehow this feels different from when we practised. The couch feels unsteady. It lurches from side to side every time Ranga turns a little. Maybe it's because James can't brace himself properly. He's flopping around a little, especially when Ranga turns left to line up the roundabout. I'm a little edgy. Apart from the dodgy steering the couch feels like it would be too heavy for just two of us to stop quickly. What if a car appears now? The noise of the skateboard wheels and James hooting drowns out any chance of hearing one coming from the side street. No. No cars are likely to be driving around here at this time of day. The streets are usually empty. We'll be right.

Still, as we approach the roundabout I lean out, trying to see around the corner. The couch is barely in control and I'm gripping the armrest as we swing wide around the centre island. James leans on Ranga and Ranga leans on me but I push back, keeping things balanced. I'm trying to look out for cars but Ranga's and James' heads are in the way so I just brace myself. Then we're through. It's not until we slow up at the bottom of the hill that I realise I've been holding my breath.

James is still hooting when we turn the couch around. He wants to go again — straightaway. Danger boy! We might have created a speed monster.

This time we're organised for the push back up the hill to the top. Ranga has some rope that we attach to the T-bar so we can steer the couch as we push it. It's not pretty but it works like a beauty — much easier than last time. All the way back up the hill James describes how good the ride was. Ranga has a huge grin on his face and I figure my smile is just as wide. This is going perfectly.

For the next run Jess gets to ride on the couch and I'm driving. I get Ranga to go down to the roundabout and look for cars. I know we won't get going as fast with only Jess pushing off but we'll still roll all the way down. Ranga reckons I'm like an old granny, worrying too much, but in the end he agrees after Jess says it's probably a good idea. No cars come while he walks down there and after a quick glance from side to side he signals. Jess starts pushing and eventually we get rolling. James just sits there as we cruise through the roundabout like a bunch of pensioners on a slow-motion Sunday drive. He's not hooting at all but he's still smiling.

Ranga walks down to us and helps me get the couch turned around. 'Well, you got down here in the end,' he says. 'What do you reckon, James?'

'It was fun,' James says, 'but the first time was way better.' As we push the couch back up the hill he tells us about all the best bits of the first run again, in detail. Ranga keeps giving me meaningful glances.

At the roundabout we check the side streets. Still nothing!

'There hasn't been a car since we started,' Ranga says, 'and there won't be one either. And what's the use of the couch if we roll so slowly that it's boring. We have to have a two-person push-off.'

I still think it's risky but Jess says that the whole point was to let James feel what skateboarding is like. She says skateboarding is a bit risky — that's what makes it so good. So finally we all agree, especially James.

'You're turning into a hoon,' I say and he laughs.

When we set up the couch for the next run Jess doesn't want to drive. 'I saw how the couch swerved from side to side when Ranga was driving. I don't reckon I'm good enough to handle it.'

I try to tell her that she's just as good as me and that she can go slow like I did, but she won't try so it's Ranga's turn to drive again.

'Go hard,' he says as Jess and I push off.

James hoots. We shove as hard as we can and then I jump into the passenger seat. This time the take-off is super fast. We're flying by the time we reach the roundabout. James is hooting his face off again, loving it, and then I see the car. Ranga's seen it too because I hear him swear. It's coming from our left and the driver hasn't seen us. Ranga tries to turn the couch away from the car just as it slams its brakes on and its tyres screech. I can't believe how loud that screech is. Then the T-bar hooks around, flicking Ranga's feet off and the couch slides across the last part of the roundabout and slams into the curb opposite. It feels like it's all happening in slow motion. I hear the wood crunch and splinter and then the couch tips up and throws me forwards. As I fall I get a glimpse of James flying off the high end of the couch. His face is pulled tight with fear like he knows what's coming but there's nothing he can do. In that split second I know that he can't move well enough to protect himself. I land in the dirt and roll. Then I'm sitting up and I hear someone whimpering. At first I think it must be James but then I realise that it's Ranga.

'Are you hurt, Ranga?'

He shakes his head. He seems frozen, curled in a ball, making a weird high moaning noise.

I look around for James. He's sprawled in a heap by the footpath on the other side of Ranga. I jump up and run over to him. He's silent, not moving, just lying there so I reach out to turn him over.

'No,' says a voice next to me. 'Don't move him. He might have spinal injuries.' It's the car driver.

The words hit me like a punch in the stomach. I feel like throwing up. I can't breathe and then Jess comes pelting down the hill, her face as white as a ghost.

The driver hands her his mobile as he crouches down

beside James. 'Ring the emergency number,' he says. 'We need an ambulance.'

It's one of those flip phones and, when she's got it open, she stares at it for a second.

'Zero, zero, zero,' the driver says. Then he goes back to James. 'Can you hear me?'

James moans a bit and nods his head.

'Good,' says the driver. 'Does anything hurt?'

I can't believe he just asked that question of a boy lying there like that. It looks like everything hurts.

James nods.

'Your back? Your neck?'

James shakes his head.

'Can you move your arms?'

James doesn't answer. He looks like he's gone to sleep. It scares me more than when he was moaning.

Carefully, the man lifts James' right leg up and tips him more onto the side. He gets one of James' hands and puts it under his cheek.

'Just lie still,' he says. 'Don't move until the ambulance drivers have checked you out.'

Ranga is still making this keening noise, hugging his knees and rocking back and forth, his eyes fixed on James.

Jess walks over and puts an arm around his shoulders.

Just to make things worse, a few big drops of rain splatter on the road while we're waiting. The sky is so dark it feels like the end of the world.

20

I've never seen Dad so angry. Mum either. They look even angrier than the sky outside.

'How could you be such an idiot?' Dad says, and they both glare at me as though I'm some sort of mass murderer. I want to try to explain how we thought we were doing something good for James and that we didn't think anything like this would happen. I think about saying how much James wanted to do it after he saw the couch, but I don't.

'Don't you realise what could have happened?' Dad doesn't wait for me to answer. 'He could have been killed. If his pump was damaged it could still do a lot of harm.'

'What really hurts,' Mum says, 'is how you deceived me. You got me to move my car out of the garage so you could fix the couch, not turn it into a skateboard. Then you wag school and now this.'

I know I should be feeling guilty but I don't, not about that anyway. Technically we did fix the couch, but I know better than to try and say that. I do feel sort of bad that I didn't tell her what we were doing, but I know if we had, she'd have stopped us. Turns out it would have been better if she had.

'It seems like every time you hang out with Warren, you do something stupid. You're grounded — and don't ask for how long! I'm too upset to make that decision at the moment.'

What? That's not fair! It's not like we planned to do anything bad. It just turned out that way.

'You're just lucky the car driver was a doctor and that girl came along when she did. Otherwise things could have worked out a whole lot worse.'

I keep my face straight. At least they won't ban me from seeing Jess if they don't know she was part of it. I don't know what to say, nothing that would help anyway, so I just keep looking at the ground.

'Look at me when I'm talking to you!' Dad yells.

I look up, but not at his face.

He lets it pass. 'We've been talking to Warren's mother and we all agree that you boys need to apologise for your stupid, irresponsible behaviour.'

I don't know where exactly this is heading but I nod to show I'm listening.

'Tomorrow, I'm taking you to the hospital. Warren will be there too. You will both say sorry to James' mother and to James for what you've done. Is that clear?' Mum's voice is low and deadly.

I nod.

Then it hits me. Ranga is supposed to be in the skateboard contest tomorrow. If we have to do this, he'll miss it.

21

When we walk in to James' hospital room, he's sitting up and his mum is in a chair beside him. Ranga and his mum are already there. All the mothers nod to each other like members of a firing squad. At least that's what I reckon, because this feels like an execution with me and Ranga as the guys who are about to be shot.

James looks at us, kind of puzzled.

Ranga's mum clears her throat. 'Do you boys have something you'd like to say to James?' She gives Ranga a shove forward.

Ranga shuffles up beside James' bed. I stand next to him.

'James,' I say, 'we'd like to apologise for our stupid behaviour. We shouldn't have put you on that couch and run you down the hill. We didn't think about the possible consequences of our actions and we're sorry you got hurt.'

James isn't looking the slightest bit serious. Even with his face all grazed up and covered in cream he's grinning. 'Are you kidding me? That was the best fun I've had in years. Thanks guys.'

Our mothers look at each other in surprise.

Beside me, Ranga takes a huge ragged breath. He's smiling but crying at the same time.

'I'm the one in hospital,' James says. 'What are you bawling about?'

Ranga grins through watery eyes. 'Nothing.'

'Does it hurt a lot?' I ask, pointing at James' face.

James shrugs. 'No more than the rest of me hurts all the time when I'm cramping. Sticks stacked it worse in the skate park, I reckon.' Saying that, he pauses for a second. 'Hey! What day is it?'

'Saturday,' I tell him.

James looks puzzled. 'Isn't the skateboard contest on today? How come you aren't there?'

Ranga smiles. 'It isn't important.'

James shakes his head. 'You would have won.'

'There's always next year,' Ranga says.

Right then, a big clap of thunder goes off and the rain that's been threatening for the last couple of days finally starts to really pelt down.

22

As soon as he gets home James comes over to my house. It's only been four days since we visited him in hospital but apart from a few scabs he looks fine. It turned out he wasn't hurt as badly as he could have been. Mum and Dad told me that if the pump had been damaged and it let go too much muscle relaxer it might have relaxed his heart because it's a muscle too. He could have died right then.

When I think about the accident I see James lying there all crumpled and covered in blood with Ranga wailing next to me. At first it felt real, like it was happening all over again, but now it's more like a bad dream. The last four days have stretched out forever. They were both hurt badly that day but James is already pretty much over it. He wants a game of Dip and Gunk.

Mum puts on the kettle for us and I'm just getting

the ramp ready for James to roll into the house when he calls, 'Hey Sticks! Ranga just ran out on the road without looking. He's coming here.'

Ranga leans over as he pelts past the letterbox. He's beaming. 'James, you're home!'

'Yeah!' says James as if it was never in doubt.

'Milo's ready, boys,' Mum calls from the kitchen. 'Oh, hello Warren. Do you want a Milo?'

'Ta, Mrs Whyte. That'd be great.' He looks nervous.

Mum gives him a big smile as though she actually likes him. 'It was nice of you to try and do something for James,' she says and then she looks around at all of us, 'but you guys should think about what might go wrong before you do anything like that again.'

We all nod together. I know I will, but I bet caution doesn't even enter Ranga's head next time he gets an idea. James' either. I just hope I can get them to listen to me.

Mum puts our cups on the table and we all sit down.

'Guess what, guys,' Ranga says. 'The contest was postponed to this weekend 'cause of the storm. Mum says I can go in it.'

James gives a hoot so loud that I jump.

23

Ranga is about to win the skateboard contest and we're all here to watch.

I can't wait to watch him go off in the final battle round! He's already blitzed the heats. No one came close even though Ranga was playing it safe. He only did the moves he can pull off one hundred per cent of the time. In the early battle rounds he pulled out some of his more technical moves. He was the best by miles but he's still got heaps left in reserve. That bully kid, Luke, has been blitzing it too but I reckon he's been skating at his limit. I don't think he can step it up from here.

Jess squeezes my hand. I've been rocking back and forth and saying, 'Come on, Ranga!' under my breath. My legs are jiggling. Jess smiles at me and I feel the grin on my face grow wider. I can't stop it, it just spreads and spreads. Could today get any better? My grin is probably at my ears by now. James must feel the same because his face is nearly splitting in half except for when one of those random expressions comes and goes.

Ranga's mum is sitting next to Mum and Dad. I think she's happy. She's smiling but her eyes are full of tears. Parents are funny like that — kind of mixed up. Mum's looking a bit teary too, but everything makes her teary, even birthdays.

Jess looks like she's about to say something when they announce the start of the final. Ranga and Luke are standing up there on the edge of the track with the officials. The judges are all there with their pads waiting. When the announcer says their names, Ranga and Luke raise their arms like they are boxers or something. Then they shake hands.

I breathe out. I kind of expected Luke to do something, but he looks okay — even friendly! Ranga is smiling too, as though he's not nervous at all, but he's scratching his arm. That's what he does when he's worried. All of a sudden a little dark cloud of doubt comes sneaking into the back of my mind. I'm trying to push it away when Luke starts his first run.

I hate to admit it but Luke goes off. He seems to have

found a new level. Everything is working. Today his airs are higher and he sticks the landings. For the whole minute of his run he flies all over the place like a pro. The judges are nodding and when he finishes everyone claps.

Then it's Ranga's turn. He stands on the edge and licks his lips. Then he tips over the edge and he's off. I feel myself relaxing. Ranga has lifted his level too. Not just one level either. He looks like something from the future. It's not just his moves, how technical they are or how high his airs are, it's how he links them together. I'm just thinking Ranga has it in the bag when he falls — hard! He's up straightaway but he's hurt his arm. He finishes his run and stands there holding it across his body. I feel sick.

When the scores are read out Luke is in front. Only by a little, but he's full of confidence. I'm thinking about what a jerk he is when he turns to Ranga. I can't hear what they are saying but Ranga shakes his head. Then Luke says something else and Ranga smiles and nods.

Then Luke starts his next run. It's almost the same as the first. He does the same moves, just in a different order. There might not be that much diversity but he kills it. He's going to get another great score.

Ranga looks nervous this time. He's flexing his hand,

making a fist and then stretching his fingers out like a starfish. He steps up to the ramp, then he looks across at all of us. We all cheer our faces off. He nods and smiles, then tips over the edge.

I shouldn't have worried. Ranga goes so high on his airs he almost goes into outer space. He invents grinds you'd think were camera tricks if they weren't in front of you and his final move was some sort of flip double-rotation that happened so fast and went so high I couldn't have even imagined it. The crowd goes ballistic as he kickflips his board into his hand and lands light as a feather on the starting platform at the end of his run. I'm cheering like a lunatic when I notice Dad doing a little war dance and punching the air. It's weird, but cool.

We have to wait for a few minutes as they tally scores but I think Ranga has won. Still anything can happen so we sit there, waiting. Finally the announcer calls Ranga and Luke up to the stage. He pauses for a moment, then declares that Ranga has the first set of perfect ten scores ever given by all the judges. He's won. The cheering and war dancing start all over again. Ranga's mum rushes up to him and hugs and kisses him, right there in front of everyone, but instead of it being uncool and embarrassing, it makes the crowd cheer even louder — even when she inspects his arm, like he's a little kid. Just like always, she's patching him up when he's hurt himself.

Then Jess is hugging me and jumping up and down at the same time. I'm hugging her back and she kisses me, in front of everyone. It's nice and I close my eyes for a moment but when I open them, over Jess' shoulder I see James looking at us. There is the saddest look on his face. It's only there for a moment. He blinks it away, smiles and gives me his version of a thumbs-up sign.

24

I stand at the edge of the skate park with my right foot on the back of my skateboard. I'm just as scared as ever but I'm not going to give up. I lean forward but my chicken legs won't push me off. I try again and they still won't obey me. Then James yells out, 'One, two, three, go!' and I do. There's a moment of panic and suddenly I'm flying up the other side. Then I manage to pull my first ever air. It's a tiny one, I know, but it feels like the biggest air ever, and I land it. I'm so shocked I just fly back up the other side and kick out.

James and Ranga are hooting and I bow. I'm getting set to go again when I feel like somebody is right behind me. I spin around and it's Luke. My eyes dart from side to side, looking for a way to escape. There isn't one. He steps closer.

'Cool move,' he says.

the end

about the author

Geoff was born in the mountains of New Guinea. As a baby he liked to sit in a sand pit on the edge of the jungle, scoffing bananas. His manners have improved a little since then. Now he likes surfing, fixing up old cars and of course, writing stories. He has been a primary school teacher for thirty-five years and thinks that is why his stories are for children. His wife says he just never grew up.

Geoff teaches at Kinross Primary School where he is always amazed at the fantastic stories the children in his class write and read to each other.

Geoff is the author of two picture books: *Ca-a-r Ca-a-a-r* (1996) and *Punzie ICQ* (1999); and several novels: *The Real Facts Of Life* (2001), *Grave of the Roti Men* (2003), *Babies Bite* (2004), *The Master* (Walker, 2009) and *Water* (Scholastic, 2010).

These days Geoff lives in Perth with his beautiful wife Sindy. Their two children, Jade and Josh, have grown up, left home and now have children of their own.

You can find out more about Geoff on his website:

www.geoffhavel.com